Shadow's

Return

Book Two

By S.C. Wynne

Chapter One

Got lots of stuff to catch up on. Probably best if I just sleep at my place tonight. T.

I stared at the note from Thompson for a good ten minutes, trying to figure out if there was a hidden meaning to it. He'd stuck the Post-it note on the coffee maker in the early dawn and crept out without waking me when he'd left for work this morning.

I poured myself a cup of coffee and added some cream. Why hadn't he woken me? Had he been trying to avoid some sort of confrontation? Did he think I'd throw a fit or something if he didn't spend the night? I squinted at the note, scanning it with my mind and wishing there was something there for me to pick up. But as usual, where Thompson was concerned, I couldn't get a reading.

We'd been pretty hot and heavy for a few months now, but nothing was written in stone. We'd both said we loved each other once, ages ago, right after we'd almost died at the hands of that pink-feather madman, Steven Pine. But since then, both of us had played it pretty close to the vest with our declarations of undying love. Had he changed his mind about me? Maybe once he'd spent some time with me doing things other than solving murders, he'd discovered I was boring. I felt boring. Maybe I wasn't inventive enough in bed? I was sort of vanilla between the sheets. I knew that. But if he wanted something more exciting, why didn't he just ask?

I sipped my coffee, feeling anxious. I missed the comfortable intimacy I'd shared with William. He'd been very verbal about his emotions, and touchy-feely. I'd had no doubt at all that William had adored me, and he'd known I'd felt the same toward him. But Thompson was more reserved, and he kept his feelings to himself. He'd admitted to never having a long-term relationship before, and sometimes that worried me. Had he stayed single for so long because he hadn't met the right person? Or was he just not relationship material?

I almost spilled my coffee when my cell rang on the counter. My stomach tensed when I saw it was Thompson himself. "Hello?" I answered.

"Liam?"

"Yep." I wasn't sure how to act suddenly. I didn't like not knowing where I stood with people. Did he sound the same as always, or was I right that he sounded more uptight?

"We have a weird one. Feel like working today?"

ust don't want you keeling over."

idn't appreciate him acting like I was a
lower. "Let's get closer to the body."
npressions seemed to blow away like
moke, and I needed to try and intercept
uickly.

rounded a stack of folding chairs, and
the victim, lying sprawled on the
ym floor. Her eyes were wide and her
n. A belt was looped around her neck,
tight the skin puckered around the
ier. My stomach rolled and I felt light-
I was damned if I was going to pass
nompson's earlier comment. I took a
and relaxed my mind, inviting the
energy in. Slowly, a replay of the
ments began to flicker in front of my
ld movie.

as smiling at someone who was just
e of my vision. Her gaze was warm
ks pink. She wasn't scared at all of
n; she was completely unaware of
ut to happen. I felt sick observing
, knowing it was about to be
en my vision skipped ahead, like a
e surface of a lake, to her screaming
un. Some guy, who had his back to
n a choke hold. She fought him
he still managed to wrap the belt
der neck.

I always preferred to work. "Sure."

"I'll swing by and get you in ten." He hung
up.

I sighed and hurried to go get dressed.
Thompson never gave me much time once he'd
actually called. I washed up, pulled on jeans and a
T-shirt, and ran my fingers through my hair. I
didn't need to look amazing; I just didn't want to
look like a hobo. I went back into the kitchen and
gulped down the rest of my coffee. I'd just set the
cup in the sink when Thompson knocked.

I opened the door and found Thompson
standing there looking tight-lipped. "Hey," I said
breathlessly, closing the door behind me. It was
strange working with the person you also slept
with. I was never sure if I should kiss him hello or
just shake hands. Today I opted for neither, and I
just followed him to the car.

I climbed in while he moved around to the
driver's side and slid in behind the wheel. I
crossed my hands in my lap, tension making my
muscles tight. "You said this was a weird one?" I
didn't look at him as I spoke, feeling oddly shy.

"It is. It's a little unsettling to be honest."

"Awesome."

"A body was discovered at Los Angeles
City College this morning." He pulled onto the
road, weaving in and out of traffic and seeming
impatient with anyone who was moving slower.

His jaw was rigid, and his brows pulled together. "Pretty gruesome."

"And it's a homicide?"

"Oh, yeah."

"Okay." I stared straight ahead. "I didn't see anything."

"That was my next question." He glanced over quickly. "I thought maybe you would."

"It's been kind of quiet to be honest." I gave a gruff laugh. I liked it when it was quiet. I needed a break from the yammering spirits and gory murders that often paraded through my brain.

"I'm glad for your peace of mind, but sorry for us. It would be helpful if you'd seen something." He sighed.

I hated disappointing him, even though it meant life was better for me. "I'm sure I'll see something when we get to the scene." My stomach tensed at the thought of what awaited me. I was happy to help the cops try and solve murders, but it wasn't for the weak of heart.

After about ten minutes, Thompson pulled into a parking lot, and we made our way across the campus. LACC wasn't a huge school, and we quickly crossed the space, passing a large tree in the center of a quad surrounded by buildings. Students sat texting on their phones and eating snacks, apparently oblivious to the fact that a murder had taken place.

"She's over there
Thompson spoke quiet

I had to hurry t
was out of breath by
gymnasium. There w
they checked our cre
One of them seemed
introduced himself t

"We've neve
happen. At least, n
looked unnerved.
handful of sexu
swallowed. "But
definitely rattled.
being stuck on
wanted to do wa
check on her.

Somethin
as we neared
under the yello
as the pressure
circulating aro
process it all a

"Anyth
through the v

"Not
forehead. "T

"You
seemed con

I sco

"I

I d
delicate f
Psychic ir
cigarette s
the spirit

We
there was
polished g
mouth ope
pulled so
brown leath
headed, bu
out after T
deep breath
surrounding
girl's last m
eyes like an

She w
out of the lin
and her chee
her companic
what was ab
her innocenc
destroyed. Th
stone across th
and trying to
me, had her
valiantly, but
around her sle

"I can't see his face," I said quickly, trying to say out loud everything that flashed in front of my eyes so Thompson could take notes. "He's wearing gloves. She's fighting him. God, she really tried to get away." My stomach lurched at how hard she'd struggled.

I'm so sorry I only see things when it's too late.

I concentrated on the vision as she clawed at her assailant. At one point she broke free and ran shrieking toward the exit. But he was faster, and he slammed her down and punched her until she was dazed and limp. Then he dragged her back to the corner where her body was now and strangled the life from her as she kicked and gasped for air.

I was so immersed in the vision, I stumbled sideways, losing my bearings. Thompson grabbed my arm. "Can you see the perp at all?"

I shook my head. "Not really. Not his face. He has red hair. From his build I'd say he's young, her age."

"Probably a student here."

The visions of her murder faded, and I inched toward the body. Usually the spirit would appear briefly and approach me with something that could be useful. We didn't have full-on conversations, but they usually dropped helpful details about their murderer. "What was her name?" I asked softly.

"Gloria." Thompson's voice was hushed.

"Gloria," I whispered, moving closer to the body. Her wide eyes and gaping mouth made my skin crawl, but I stayed near her, reminding myself that that was just her shell, and that her spirit was around here somewhere. "Talk to me, Gloria." There was nothing. "Come on, let us help you find justice."

"Maybe it's too late." Thompson sounded resigned.

"Shhh."

He grunted.

"Gloria, tell me who did this to you." I pressed my fingers to my temple. "Please help us. Don't let him get away with this."

I winced when she appeared in front of me like a sickly hologram, her skin gray and her confusion palpable. "I don't understand. I just wanted someone to listen." Her voice was weak and reedy.

"Okay." I nodded. "Well, I'm listening."

"I didn't mean it." She whimpered. "I didn't want that. Not really."

"Didn't want what?" I nudged.

She frowned and touched her neck. "Not fair. Not fair."

"Can you give me details, Gloria?"

Her mouth was a grim line. "Tricked me."

"Give me his name." Even I could hear the urgency in my voice. She wasn't going to stay long, and I needed a name if she had one.

"Pine. Pine. Pine. Pine."

"Pine? Like the tree?" I struggled with understanding her fragmented sentences.

"He said he was my friend."

"Who?"

"I didn't do anything to him. Why?"

"Do you have a name for me, Gloria? Is Pine the name of a person?"

"The angel made him do it," she said, and then she disappeared.

"Gloria?" I called her name even though I knew she was gone. Her energy had evaporated completely.

Thompson grabbed my arm. "What? What did she say? Did you get a name?"

"Maybe." I turned my confused gaze on him. "She… she said Pine."

"I thought that was what you said." He grimaced, looking nonplussed. "She actually said the word 'pine'?"

"Yes. But she was all over the place. It might have just been a tree for all I know." My stomach clenched with an uneasy feeling.

"You're sure she said pine?"

"I just said I was."

"Well…" He scratched his head. "What else did she say?"

I sighed. "She felt betrayed. That was very obvious." I squinted. "And she said something about an angel making him do it."

"An angel?" Thompson scowled.

I couldn't shake a feeling of apprehension shrouding me. "He… he said something about being an angel. Remember?"

"He? You mean Steven Pine?" Thompson's face tensed. "Liam, he's in jail."

"Yeah. I know. But he's also the strongest fucking psychic I've ever met. Maybe he can reach out somehow." I shivered and hugged myself.

"She must have got it wrong."

I rubbed my stomach, feeling queasy. "Why would she just pull that name out of the blue? Spirits don't lie, and they don't make stuff up."

"Well, they can make mistakes, right? Perhaps she likes pine trees."

"She didn't say it in a happy way."

"Okay. Maybe she read about Steven Pine. His case has been all over the news. Maybe he was on her mind when she died."

"It felt more personal."

"But you saw the murderer. He had red hair, and he was young. That's what you said."

"I know—" I frowned, trying to push away the chill that seemed embedded in my soul.

He raked a hand through his shaggy hair. "No way they let that nutcase out. You're letting your imagination run wild." He pulled his cell from his pocket and walked away with it pressed to his ear.

I moved away from the body. Gloria wouldn't return, and I needed fresh air. I followed Thompson toward the exit, still feeling shaken. Maybe Thompson was right and I was letting my fear of Steven Pine get to me. He'd been a terrifying foe, and his name had been all over the newspapers recently because his lawyers were trying to hold up his trial with bogus legal technicalities. The Steven Pine case had been horrifyingly personal. He'd dragged me into his murderous rampage, and I guess it was possible I'd let the memory of that case seep into my current work.

Thompson hung up and faced me. "He's still at Men's Central, just like I thought."

I squinted back toward the building we'd just left. "Okay." I still felt uneasy. I'd never dealt with a psychic quite like Steven. I wasn't really sure what he was capable of.

"I'm going to touch base with a few other people before we leave." His gaze was emotionless.

"Go for it."

While Thompson finished talking to anyone who'd been first on the scene, I stood to the side, trying to remember every detail of my interaction with Gloria and typing it into the notepad app on my phone. There had been no witnesses to the actual murder. The school janitor had found the body when he'd opened up the gym early this morning. He'd said the place was locked and that there was no one around. The cops took his prints just to rule him out as a suspect, but I knew already he wasn't our guy.

Eventually, Thompson indicated that he was ready to head out. We walked to his car in silence and got in without a word. I didn't bring up anything about how I felt like he was acting odd. I didn't have the nerve to open that can of worms yet. He drove to the station, where he could write up a report and get the names and addresses of Gloria's friends and family. The sooner we could talk to the people closest to her, the better.

I watched Thompson at his desk as he called people and set up meetings for later in the day. I didn't like feeling uncertain about what we had. But the way he'd just left that note and not said goodbye this morning wasn't like him. If there was one thing Thompson was, it was predictable. Whenever he deviated from his usual behavior, there was always a reason.

I had no idea what could have changed between now and last night. Everything had seemed just fine last evening. We'd talked a little bit about William because I'd come across an old photo album, and then we'd had dinner, fucked, and gone to bed. Everything had been pretty damn perfect.

He cleared his throat. "I'm going to interview Gloria's boyfriend. Did you want to tag along?"

I frowned. "Of course." I always came with him on those sorts of interviews. Why was he suddenly questioning that?

He stood, pulling on his blazer. "I just wasn't sure if you'd want to."

"Since when?"

He shrugged and moved toward the exit. I hurried after him, feeling confused. When we got to the elevator it was crowded, so I couldn't really ask him anything. By the time we got to his car, enough time had passed that it felt awkward to bring up how weird he was being, but I decided to do it anyway. Just like Thompson was always predictable, I was usually awkward.

As he pulled out of the parking structure, I shifted to face him. "Is something bugging you?"

He glanced at me, his expression guarded. "What do you mean?"

"You seem different."

"I do?" He kept his eyes on the road.

"Why did you leave a note on the coffee maker?"

"Did you not want me to leave you a note?"

I sighed. "You didn't say goodbye. You always say goodbye."

A muscle in his jaw tensed. "I didn't want to wake you. You were deeply asleep, and you have trouble sleeping."

"So you were just being considerate?"

"Yep."

"Promise?"

"If you want me to wake you up next time, I will."

His tone was evasive, and I was even more convinced that something was wrong. But I didn't know how to really dig deeper if he was going to pretend everything was perfect. I didn't want to come off like some drama queen or anything like that.

"I don't know. You just seem different."

He cleared his throat. "We should probably focus on the case."

My face warmed at his lecturing tone. "I am focused on the case." He didn't need to tell me how to do my part of the job. He was definitely deflecting. God, what the hell could be so awful that he didn't even want to talk about it? I knew I wasn't the most normal person in the world, but I didn't think I'd done anything that would make him want to stop seeing me.

"I'm just saying we can talk about... us... later," he said quietly.

"Fine by me."

His hands clenched on the steering wheel as he gave a hard laugh. "I have to say it's shocking that you'd be the one to want to talk about feelings."

"Trust me; it's not that I *want* to talk about that stuff."

"Then let's not."

"Sounds good." I clamped my jaw. Did he want to see other people and he didn't know how to bring it up? The thought of that made my stomach ache. My feelings for Thompson hadn't lessened. If anything they were stronger. But the way he was acting, there was no way I'd share that tidbit with him.

After a few minutes he said, "Did you know you talk in your sleep?"

I frowned. "I do?"

"Yes."

"Huh. Well, if I said I wanted to sleep with Ryan Reynolds or something, don't hold that against me."

He parked in front of an apartment building where presumably Gloria's boyfriend lived. He shut the engine off and turned to face me. "Ryan Reynolds I could compete with."

I smirked. "Is that right? You have a pretty high opinion of yourself."

"I'm not worried about you fantasizing about movie stars."

"Okay." I laughed, feeling confused. "That's good because I'm sure there will be more dreams about Ryan and others. I can't control my dreams."

"I know," he said softly. "You have no control over how you feel or who you love. I know that."

I love you, Thompson.

Those four words were right there on the tip of my tongue. I could have said them so easily. I did love him. But he was acting so odd — no way was I showing my soft underbelly right now. Maybe his whole "you have no control over who you love" speech was the one he gave all the people he dumped. Was that what was happening here? Was he trying to break up with me, but it was extra awkward because we worked together?

My pride warred with my desire to keep seeing him. On one level, I wanted to protect my heart, but on another, I really didn't want to lose him. It had been a long time since I'd had to even think about things like this. I'd had such an easy, stable relationship with Will from the very beginning. I wasn't used to playing the dating game anymore.

I met his gaze, my heart rate elevated. "We should probably go talk to this boyfriend of Gloria's."

His face tensed. "Yeah." He turned away to open his door. "Let's do that."

I climbed out of the car, feeling like I'd dodged a bullet but not sure that had been the best thing. If Thompson was having second thoughts about us, we'd need to address that. But I shoved those thoughts away for now.

S.C. Wynne

Chapter Two

We headed up the stairs at the end of the apartment complex. "What's the number of the apartment?" I asked.

"208."

I led the way, which was not really how this usually went. As we neared the door, I backed off, letting Thompson take the lead. If Gloria's boyfriend was the killer, I didn't need to be leading the charge.

Thompson rapped his knuckles on the door. When no one answered, he knocked again, and this time a dark-haired guy opened the door, looking annoyed. "What?" he snapped. His expression changed when he saw Thompson. Thompson didn't need a uniform to give off a cop vibe. "Sorry. Can I help you?"

"Are you Kyle Clark?"

"Yes."

Thompson flashed his badge, and the guy seemed to wilt. "I'm Detective Thompson, and this is Liam Baker. Do you think we could have a word?"

The guy nodded and stepped back into his apartment, and we followed him in, leaving the door ajar. He crossed his arms and shifted uneasily. "If this is about those parking tickets, I was going to pay them today."

Kyle was easy to read—he'd had zero intention of paying any tickets today or any other day. The image of a sizable bag of weed stuffed in a suitcase came to me. He was trying to throw us off by mentioning the parking tickets because he had pot in his apartment. He desperately hoped Thompson and I wouldn't notice the bong he had next to the couch.

"I'm afraid our visit is concerning something more serious." Thompson sounded matter-of-fact. I wasn't sure how he stayed so calm and unruffled when telling loved ones that their person was gone. I always felt sweaty and nervous when we had to deliver that kind of news, but Thompson seemed to take it in stride.

Kyle frowned. "Serious how?"

Thompson didn't answer the question; instead he asked his own. "Are you in a relationship with a Gloria Handy?"

"Yeah. Why?" Kyle flicked his gaze between Thompson and me.

"I regret to inform you Gloria was found murdered this morning." Thompson's gaze was pinned on Kyle, watching for any tells that might give us a clue as to his guilt or innocence.

Kyle's explosive emotions came at me like a wave, and I winced at the grief that washed over me, grunting audibly. He clutched his head and stared at us as if he couldn't believe his ears.

"No. No. That can't be true." His voice shook, and his eyes were wide. "I don't fucking believe you."

"I'm sorry," Thompson said quietly.

Kyle sat quickly on the couch, still staring. "But how? Why?"

Again, Thompson didn't answer Kyle's questions. "When was the last time you saw Gloria?"

He blinked a few times, still looking shaken. "God, I don't know... Yesterday, I guess."

"You guess?"

Kyle grimaced. "Yesterday. Sorry. We saw each other before her psychology class."

"Did you two argue about anything?"

He scowled. "What? No!" He stood again, looking like he'd love to bolt out the door behind me. "Are you trying to pin this on me?"

"We're just asking some questions, Kyle. Calm down." Thompson's voice was even.

"Yeah, I know how you guys work." Kyle raked a hand through his hair. "I loved Gloria. There's no way I'd hurt her."

"Where were you last night?"

"Here." His gaze almost slid to the bong, but he caught himself. "I was tired and I stayed in."

"Anyone see you who can corroborate that?" Thompson tugged his little notepad from his breast pocket. "Maybe you had a few friends over?"

"I was alone."

That wasn't good for him. The boyfriends and spouses were always the first people the cops suspected. I knew Thompson was a fair-minded person, but the cold hard fact was that 55 percent of all murders of women in the US were committed by intimate partners.

"No one saw you or talked to you at all?" I spoke up, nudging him. My senses told me he wasn't our guy. "Maybe you talked to someone on the phone or something like that?"

Thompson shot me a funny look. I don't think he was pleased that I was trying to help Kyle.

Kyle nodded slowly. "I did talk to my mom."

"When?" Thompson asked curtly.

"Shit, I think it was like ten at night?" He sighed. "I was kind of out of it." He cleared his throat. "I'd had a few beers."

Right. Beers.

"So you never left the apartment all evening?" Thompson asked.

"No." Kyle frowned.

Thompson gave me a questioning glance, and I nodded. He sighed. "I'm going to need you to come down to the station later today so we can print you."

Kyle's eyes were red-rimmed, and he looked like he was about to burst into tears. "Is this really happening?"

My stomach clenched with empathy for the kid.

"I'm afraid so." Thompson twisted his lips as he studied Kyle. "You said Gloria had a psychology class?"

Kyle nodded. "Yeah."

"Did she have any other classes last night?"

"No. Wednesdays she just has — had — that one class." He looked queasy.

Why had she been in the gymnasium if she only had a psychology class? Had the killer kidnapped her and dragged her there? I remembered how relaxed she'd looked in the first part of my vision, and it was clear to me that she'd gone with that person willingly. "How were you and Gloria doing relationship-wise?" I asked.

Kyle glanced up uneasily. "Pretty good."

"How long had you been together?"

Shrugging, Kyle said, "We've been together off and on since high school."

"More off than on?" I asked.

Kyle looked apprehensive.

"When you say pretty good, that makes me think maybe you guys had a few issues," Thompson said, scribbling something on his pad.

"Not really. I mean, no one gets along all the time." Kyle licked his lips nervously. "Right?"

I thought about how weird things were between Thompson and me at the moment, and I winced. "Definitely not."

Thompson studiously avoided my gaze. "What kind of problems did you and Gloria have?"

Kyle stared down at his clasped hands. "Just typical couple stuff."

"Elaborate," growled Thompson. "Now is not the time to be evasive."

He sighed. "She wanted to move in together, and I wasn't quite there yet." His face crumpled suddenly, and a sob tore from his throat. "God, would she be alive if I'd said yes?" He looked at us with his bloodshot eyes.

"There's no way to know that." I felt compelled to comfort him.

"How... how did she die?" His lower lip trembled.

I was aware that what he really wanted to know was whether or not she'd suffered. Her death certainly hadn't been an easy one. I hated that I couldn't tell him she'd died peacefully. "She was strangled," I said quietly.

He winced. "Oh, Jesus. Fuck. *Why?*" His pain was raw and convincing. It ate at my gut and made my chest hurt. "She was the sweetest girl."

"I'm sorry."

Thompson shifted. "Can you think of anyone who'd want to hurt Gloria? Maybe an ex who couldn't let go, or a coworker she had problems with."

"No. Everybody loved Gloria." He closed his eyes.

Not quite everybody.

Thompson pulled a card from his pocket and set it on the coffee table in front of Kyle. "Like I said, we need you to come down and get printed. We also may need to ask you some more questions when we have more information on things like time of death."

Kyle's shoulders slumped, and he didn't look up. "Of course."

Thompson moved to the door, and I followed. Glancing back at Kyle, I watched his shoulders shake as he covered his face and let loose his grief. I closed the door, almost embarrassed to have witnessed his breakdown.

Thompson and I made our way to the car in silence. Once we were on the road, he sighed. "He didn't do it, did he?"

"I don't see how. He looks nothing like the guy, and he'd have to be the best damn liar I've ever met. There were no guilty thoughts or anything like that. I just sensed heartbreak."

"Hopefully we'll have time of death by tomorrow at the latest. We need to narrow the time window, and that will narrow our list of suspects. At the moment it could be anybody who was on campus last night. That's a big group."

"Yeah." I leaned back against the seat. "So who do we talk to next?"

"I think we should speak with her parents. Grab the folder behind the seat, would you?"

I did as requested. "Why didn't we do that first?"

"I had a black and white deliver the bad news. I thought it was more important to see her boyfriend's face when he found out Gloria was dead."

"He was devastated."

"Yeah. Even I could see that." He didn't sound pleased. I couldn't blame him. It was in his nature to catch the bad guy as quickly as possible.

I riffled through the sheets of paper. "Gloria's mom died last year of cancer."

"Seriously?"

"Yeah. Looks like her dad is still in the picture, thank goodness."

"Jesus, that family is having a run of bad luck. Any siblings?"

"No."

"God." He exhaled roughly. "Her poor father."

I studied him out of the corner of my eye, trying not to be noticed. He didn't usually let the job get to him, so I wasn't sure what was different about today. Maybe because the victim was only eighteen? Or maybe it was because we were at odds, and that unsettled him. I really, really wished I could read Thompson whenever I wanted. But I just got occasional glimpses that didn't really give me what I craved. If his mind had been open to me, then I'd have felt better about things between us. I didn't enjoy having to guess what he felt about me. I hated having to figure all of this out like regular people.

I grimaced and tried to focus on the case. "Have there been any other homicides like this one lately? Anyone strangled with a belt recently?" I squinted at him.

"Nothing comes to mind. But it's not like I know every single case off the top of my head."

"I'd love to know exactly what she meant when she said the word 'pine.'" I stared out the window morosely. The neighborhood we were in was pretty high-end. The houses were all sprawling mansions, with perfect lawns and fancy cars in the driveways.

"We both know there's no way Steven Pine killed her."

"Yeah. I know. But it's weird that she said that. Of all the words she could have used."

"Maybe you heard her wrong." He gave me a quick glance.

"No. I heard her just fine."

He shrugged. "Well, her murderer wasn't Steven Pine."

We pulled up to ornate iron gates. Thompson spoke into the little metal squawk box on his side, explaining who we were. After a few seconds, the gates swung wide and we drove through to park in front of a big colonial home. We made our way to the door, and when it opened, an elderly woman stood there looking grim.

"I'm Detective Thompson, and this is my associate, Liam Baker." He flashed his badge, not giving any real details about just what type of associate I was.

"Come in." She stepped aside, her jaw tight. "My son is in the library."

Once we were inside, Thompson studied her. "You're Gloria's grandmother?"

"Yes. I'm Alicia Handy." She looked like maybe she'd been crying; her eyes were red and puffy. "I still can't believe it." She stopped talking and gave a little choking sound.

She wasn't super easy to read. I could feel her pain, but it was confusing as to whether she was grieving for her son's loss or if she was actually heartbroken about Gloria's death. She put a well-manicured hand to her silky gray hair as she led us across the marble foyer toward what was most likely the library. She pushed open the large mahogany doors, and we entered the dark room.

A fire crackled across the room, but there were no lights on and the curtains were closed. It was hard to see, but I made out the shape of a man sitting in an armchair in front of the hearth.

"The police are here, Alex." Her voice wobbled. "Again."

Turning his head slowly, the man stood. "Come in."

We approached, and I winced at the level of agony he gave off. I had to catch my breath his pain was so intense.

Alicia switched on a side table lamp, and Alex held up his hand, grimacing. But he didn't say anything; he just lowered his hand as if in a stupor. "What can I do for you?" His voice was monotone.

"First of all, we're very sorry for your loss," Thompson said gruffly.

"Thanks." Alex sounded like a robot.

"Would you mind telling us when you last saw your daughter?" Thompson asked.

Alicia spoke briskly, before Alex could answer. "Why don't we sit?" She perched on the edge of a chair near her son, and he sat again, where he'd been before. She waved to the two chairs across from them. "Sit. Please."

I was able to sense Thompson's impatience. He didn't want to sit and have a nice visit; he wanted to jump into the questions right away. But he lowered himself into one of the chairs and plastered on a polite expression. "So, when did you last see Gloria?"

Alex shuddered. "Two days ago."

I frowned. "Didn't she live here?"

"Yes," Alex said quietly. "But she stays with that boyfriend of hers a lot of the time. Stayed. She… she stayed with him a lot."

Alicia swallowed loudly. "I don't know why. He lives in a horrible area. I wouldn't be surprised if one of his low-life friends followed her and—" She gulped.

Alex grimaced. "Mother, please."

Her frustration came at me like a wave of warm water. She'd disliked Kyle and been upset with Gloria. But her anger was just your typical family type; it wasn't a murderous rage. She'd been disappointed in her granddaughter's choice of men, but not to the extent that she'd have harmed her.

"Well, it's the truth. I warned her that he was no good for her, but she just couldn't seem to stay away." Alicia wrung her hands. "And now she's gone."

Alex's face crumpled, and he started crying.

I froze, meeting Thompson's uncomfortable gaze. We needed to talk to Alex and, as awkward as this was, we couldn't just leave and let him grieve in private. Not yet. "She's at peace now." I spoke quickly, not even sure what it was I wanted to say to him. I simply needed Alex to know that she wasn't suffering anymore. Maybe then he'd be able to talk to us and tell us details about Gloria's life. Because that was where we'd find the murderer; in the details.

Alex looked up, his face wet and pasty. "Are you a priest?"

I shook my head. "No. I'm... I'm a psychic."

Alicia scrunched her face in distaste. "A psychic? What in the world are you doing here?"

Thompson cleared his throat. "We use Liam to help us solve difficult cases."

"Do you use a crystal ball?" Alicia looked puzzled.

"No. But I can sense things. Especially if I touch items from the victim. Sometimes there are traces of their life lingering and I can pick up clues."

Alex sniffed, looking less freaked-out than his mother. "Can you sense Gloria right now?"

I couldn't. I couldn't sense her presence here in this house at all. But I didn't want to tell them that. "Maybe if I could see her room?"

Alicia scowled. "Well, why?"

"As I said before, so that I can touch something of hers." I hoped I didn't sound like a creeper. Most people really didn't understand my gift. I couldn't blame them, not after all the nutty stuff Hollywood came up with about psychics.

"Do you see the future?" Alicia asked.

"No. I see the past."

"Well, what good is that?" she asked gruffly.

"It comes in handy when someone's been murdered." Thompson's deep voice cut across the space. "It's kind of a way of interviewing them after their death."

Alicia touched her chest. "Oh. I didn't think of that."

I shrugged. "You're not alone. A lot of people think seeing the future is the only thing psychics do."

"So then... you saw... what happened to Gloria?" Alex asked, his expression weary.

"I did."

"My God," Alex whimpered.

"Do you already know who did it?" Alicia looked confused. "Because if that's the case, why are you here?"

I grimaced. "I couldn't see the perpetrator's face. I'm sorry." I turned to Alex. "We're here to try and connect with Gloria. On a psychic level."

"Oh," Alex said.

"Which is why I'd like to see Gloria's room."

Alex nodded slowly. "Okay. I don't mind if you do that."

"Are you sure, son?" Alicia looked alarmed. "Do you really want them tramping through her room?"

"We'll be respectful," Thompson said, reassuringly. "It might be very helpful to the investigation if Liam could see her room."

Alex stood suddenly, looking hopeful. "Yes. Anything to find this monster who hurt my little girl."

My heart ached for him, but I tried to keep my face blank and my emotions in check. The last thing anybody needed was me crying and weeping along with the family. I met Thompson's blank stare. "That would be great," I said softly.

"This all seems very odd to me." Alicia pulled her dark brows together.

Alex ignored her and led the way out of the library. His steps were quick, as if he was almost excited about showing us Gloria's room. Once we were at the top of the stairs, Alex hesitated outside one of the doors. He glanced at me, his eyes glittering. "I loved my daughter. I hope you can sense that."

I nodded because I definitely could.

"Her mother died. Did you know that?"

"Yes."

He pressed his hand to the door, lowering his head. "Gloria tried to kill herself a few months ago." He looked up, his eyes feverish. "But I found her in time and saved her." A sob rumbled through him.

"I'm so sorry," I muttered as a tear slipped from my eye. I was embarrassed to be emotional, but his pain was so raw it was as if I was experiencing it with him.

"I wish I could have saved her again." His lips quivered as tears dribbled down his pale cheeks.

"I know."

"I was self-absorbed because of her mom." He pushed the door open, and he gave me a weak smile. "But we had such a good talk the last time I saw her."

"I'm glad."

He wiped his face with the back of his arms. "Yes. She explained why she did it."

"It's good you two could clear the air."

"Yes." Exhaling, he said, "She told me she just wanted someone to listen. And once she finally had that, she said she felt much better. Hopeful even."

I remembered when I'd connected with her earlier, she'd mentioned wanting someone to listen. If she'd been referring to her suicide attempt, I wasn't sure why she'd have brought that up at the scene of her murder. Generally things the spirits said were designed to help me solve their death. Her death certainly hadn't been a suicide. "I'm glad you were able to give her what she needed."

Alex sighed and stepped aside for us to enter the room. "I wish I could take credit for that. But I travel all the time with work, and I'm afraid I fell short in the nurturing department most of the time."

I entered her bedroom, taking in the pink rug and wall paper. "Oh, I thought you said she'd found someone to listen."

"She did." He grimaced. "But it wasn't me."

S.C. Wynne

Chapter Three

"She'd joined a suicide support group at school." He looked guilty.

"I see." I nodded.

"I handled my grief of losing her mother poorly and wasn't really able to empathize with what she was going through. Losing a wife is different from losing your mother. I didn't know how to help her. The group had people her age who understood her struggle on a personal level."

Thompson perked up. "Would you happen to have the name or contact info for the person who ran the group?"

"I don't. Sorry."

"Even a first name would be helpful," Thompson coaxed.

Alex shrugged. "I don't think she ever told me any names."

Thompson sighed impatiently at his answer. "I suppose I can get the name of the group leader from the school."

"I know it wasn't a big group," Alex offered.

"Thanks," Thompson murmured.

Alex winced as he glanced around his daughter's room. "I can't believe she's gone. I remember when we decorated this room. She was ten, and everything had to be pink. Absolutely everything." He turned his sad gaze on me. "Do you feel anything from being in here?"

"Not yet."

He sighed and inched toward the door. "Do you mind if I just leave you to it? I can't be in here. I thought maybe it would make me feel better, but it doesn't."

"Of course. We'll be down in just a bit." Thompson moved to the door. Once Alex was gone, he closed the door and turned to me. "We need the name of whoever ran that group."

"I agree. Even if they didn't hurt Gloria, the members in that club might have information that's helpful." I ran my hand along her comforter, opening my senses.

"And most importantly, you can scan their brains for info."

"Yeah. If I can connect to them." Sometimes Thompson made me feel like one of those gadgets at the grocery store that read the UPC labels on canned goods.

"I have faith in you."

"Thanks."

I didn't feel any vibrations near her bed, so I moved toward her dresser. There were little brown and white cat figurines on the top of the dresser, and when I picked up one of them something buzzed through me. I saw Gloria laughing and leaning in to kiss someone. Once again, I only saw the back of the person's head, and they had on a knit cap, so I couldn't see their hair color. The memory faded, and I scowled. "I think Gloria was cheating on Kyle."

"Why do you say that?" His gaze was sharp.

"I just saw her kissing some guy, and it wasn't Kyle. I could tell from the body type it wasn't Kyle. Too slender."

He narrowed his eyes. "Was it the killer's body type?"

"Possibly." I was frustrated the vision had been so fleeting. It hadn't given me time to search for things like moles, tattoos, or little defining details.

"If Gloria was cheating, that might give Kyle a motive for murder."

"Yep. Except I didn't get that sense from Kyle. I don't think he suspected she was cheating on him."

"Maybe she wasn't cheating. Maybe she was just really affectionate."

"Perhaps. But in the vision I had at the scene, she looked kind of like someone looks when they're attracted. You know, flushed cheeks and shining eyes."

"Got it." Thompson was going through the drawers of her desk. He seemed frustrated as he riffled through the contents. He held up a handful of pink pens. "How many pens does one girl need?"

I glanced over. "Yeah. Really. It seems like nobody even writes longhand anymore." I frowned as a thought occurred to me. "Hey, did you guys find her cell phone on her?"

"No. Her purse was there with her ID, but not her phone."

I frowned. "Well, that's odd. Kids her age always have their phones on them."

"Yeah. I thought the same thing."

"So maybe whomever killed her stole it because it had information about them on it."

"It's a possibility." He straightened. "Things were easier when people wrote on paper. I miss the days when I could look through a damn drawer and find a pad with some clues on it. Now everything is on the damn electronic devices, and if you can't find those, you're screwed."

I smirked. "Were you hoping to pull a Barnaby Jones?"

He scowled. "What?"

"You know, where he'd rub a pencil over the notepad in the victim's home and it would reveal the phone number of the bad guy?"

"Ha. Ha."

"Hey, it worked for him."

"You do realize Barnaby Jones wasn't a real detective, right?"

"Gasp."

His lips twitched. "You're hysterical, Liam. How about you be quiet and let a real detective work?"

"You mean like Rockford?"

He snorted.

I glanced at Gloria's desk. "Shouldn't someone her age have a laptop or a tablet or something?"

"You would think so."

"So then, where is it?"

He crossed his arms, glancing over at me. "Not here."

"Yeah."

He sighed. "Since there doesn't seem to be any physical evidence for me to find, would you please use your magical mojo to figure something out for us? Because so far all we have is maybe she was cheating on her boyfriend."

"I'll do my best." I returned to the cat statues, since that was really the only place I'd felt any connection to Gloria. I fingered a couple of other figurines, closing my eyes and trying to be open. After about five minutes, I was ready to give up, and Thompson's phone buzzed.

"Hello." His voice was hushed, as if he didn't want to disturb me. Little did he know I wasn't having any luck anyway. "What?" His voice was sharp.

I moved toward him, wondering what had him agitated.

"I'll be right there." He hung up and met my curious gaze. "The coroner found something interesting." He led the way out of the room. Alicia met us at the foot of the stairs. "Thanks for letting us look around."

She smiled coolly. "I can only hope you put things back the way you found them."

"Of course," Thompson said, unruffled by her snooty tone. "Can you tell Alex goodbye for us? We need to head back to the station."

"No problem," she cooed.

We left the big house and got in the car. Thompson started the engine and backed up all the way down the long driveway. I had to admire his driving skills; I'd have probably ended up in the rosebushes if I'd tried that maneuver.

"So what did the coroner find?" I urged. I was a little annoyed Thompson wasn't just telling me without my asking.

He guided the car through the iron gates and then pulled onto the main highway. "She found a note in the victim's mouth."

My pulse spiked a little. "She did?"

"Yep."

"What did it say?"

"I don't know yet. I guess we'll see when we get there."

I settled into the seat. "We should talk to some of Gloria's friends from school next. They'll probably know details about the suicide support group."

"I have about five of them coming in this afternoon."

"You're not wasting any time."

"No." He sighed. "Cases that involve kids her age put a real fire under my ass."

"Yeah. It's not like I don't care about all our cases. But when it's young adults who haven't even lived life, it's harder to take."

He grunted and after a while we reached the medical examiner's office. It was housed in a big red building that had originally been built in 1912 and was part of the county hospital's old administration building. I couldn't walk into that old place without spirits coming at me in droves. I hated visiting the ME for that very reason.

As we walked the corridors, three spirits screeched at me about how they'd been murdered. I felt bad ignoring them, but I couldn't deal with them at the moment. I winced and exhaled roughly, the stress of their raised voices getting to me.

Thompson glanced over. "You okay?"

"Just a lot of angry spirits giving me an earful."

He surprised me when he put his arm around my shoulders. It took a lot of control not to show my astonishment. He glanced around the empty hallway with a dirty look. "Back off, assholes." His voice rumbled in his chest. "He's with me."

I laughed because the idea of Thompson trying to defend me from invisible assailants amused me. "It's okay. I'm used to it." Maybe I was acting tough, but I liked the feel of his arm hooked around me. It was comforting. And for whatever reason, the spirits did seem to fade slightly the second he touched me.

"I don't like it when you turn white and look nauseous."

I frowned. "I didn't realize I did that."

"Yep. Every time we come in this building, you look like you're about to puke." He grinned down at me.

My pulse stuttered at his warm smile. After how distant he'd been earlier, I was happy to feel a connection with him again. I felt slightly pathetic that I was that desperate for his attention, but it was what it was.

Once we reached the office of the ME, he dropped his arm. The spirits immediately came back, hissing about their need for justice. I ignored them, and we waited for the coroner to come talk with us. When she appeared, she looked harassed with her cheeks flushed and her glasses askew. She carried two plastic bags as she approached.

"Thompson." She smiled at him and gave me a curt nod. I knew that I made her squeamish, which was funny considering she worked with dead bodies all day. Without any wasted pleasantries, she launched into giving us information. "Rigor had set in by the time this girl was found, but putrefaction hadn't begun. Based on body temperature, I'm putting her time of death between 9:00 p.m. and 6:00 a.m. There was no sign of sexual assault. We did find tissue under her fingernails, and I've sent it to the lab. Hopefully there will be some usable DNA there that's helpful in pinpointing her killer."

"If he's in the database," I said softly.

"That would be nice." Thompson rubbed the back of his neck. "So you said you found a note in the victim's mouth?"

"It's not a note exactly." She grimaced and held out one of the bags she had.

Thompson took the bag and squinted. "Looks like a questionnaire of some kind."

"Yes. But very bizarre questions."

Fingering the plastic, Thompson read aloud. "Are you happy? Do you trust me? Do you believe in fate?" He scrunched his face into a frown. "What the hell kind of questions are those?"

"That's what I thought too. Very odd." The coroner widened her eyes.

"And stuffing that in her mouth just makes this even weirder," I addressed Thompson.

"But I'm afraid it gets stranger." The coroner held out a second plastic baggie. "This was also in her mouth. But it was almost down her throat. I missed it on the first go around."

A chill went through me as I saw the pink feather encased in the bag. "Thompson." My voice was hard.

"Yeah." He grabbed the bag, scowling.

"My first thought, naturally, was your old friend Pine." The coroner glanced around and lowered her voice. "But of course, that's impossible."

"It is impossible," Thompson said gruffly. "He's in jail."

"Copycat?" she asked. "It wouldn't be the first time."

"It has to be." My voice was emotionless. "He can't kill people from jail. That's not physically possible." I felt shaky as I stared at the feather.

"No. Certainly not." She nodded.

I shivered. "Besides, I saw the actual killer."

"You did?" She perked up. "Oh, well that's a lucky break."

I sighed. "I just saw him from behind. But I got a good enough look to know it wasn't Pine."

"Well, of course it wasn't. A person can't be in two places at once." She laughed uneasily.

Thompson gave me a stern look. "Liam, it's a copycat. That's all it is."

I knew he had to be right, but I couldn't shake the feeling of doom and gloom hanging over me. "I know that logically."

The coroner shifted restlessly. "I have a lot of work so..."

"Of course." Thompson nodded. Once she was gone, he turned to me. "We should catalog this evidence and go talk to Gloria's friends."

"Okay." I hugged myself, glancing apprehensively at the pink feather. "Anyone could know about that detail. It was in all the papers."

"Exactly." Thompson led the way from the building. Once in the car, Thompson handed the plastic bags to me. I held them on my lap, looking at them like they were rattlesnakes. He sighed. "Shouldn't you touch them and try to get something off of them?"

"Yes." I didn't move.

He gave a gruff laugh. "Like, in the near future."

My stomach clenched as I picked up the bag with the note. I closed my eyes and waited for something to come to me. When nothing did, I frowned and looked at Thompson. "That's weird. I didn't get anything."

"Really?" A deep line appeared between his brows. "Try the feather."

I switched bags and tried again, but still no information came to me at all. I scowled and met Thompson's puzzled gaze. "It's like they've been washed of all psychic clues."

"Is that a thing?" he asked.

"Not really." The only time I'd experienced anything close was dealing with the prostitutes Steven Pine had murdered. He'd been able to block me from information when he wanted. "You probably know what I'm going to say next."

"Liam." He sounded frustrated. "We need to focus on this case and stop worrying about Pine."

His annoyance was painted with uneasiness. I wasn't even sure he recognized that he was as freaked-out about all the clues leading back to Pine's case as I was. "I am working this case. I'm doing what you ask of me. I can't help it if everything keeps pointing back to *him*."

"It's coincidence. At most what we have here is a copycat killer."

"Sure. Only this last murder wasn't really a copycat in that she wasn't a prostitute. She was just an average college student, brutally murdered." I hesitated. "With a pink feather stuffed in her mouth." I shivered.

"So the guy is a lousy copycat. Not all criminals are smart, and he probably wanted to put his own spin on things."

"By targeting non-prostitutes."

"Exactly."

"I guess." I pressed the bag with the feather to my forehead.

Nothing.

"This is so fucking weird." I scowled at the feather.

Thompson put the car in reverse and then pulled out onto the road. "Let's just go back to the station and talk to Gloria's friends. Someone will have something for us, I'm sure of it."

"Maybe you should take over the psychic duties."

He sighed. "Come on, Liam."

I slid down in the seat. "What the hell good am I if I can't get the info we need?"

"First of all, you got plenty this morning at the scene." He kept his eyes on the road. "And secondly... we make a good team."

I was surprised at his statement. Pleasantly surprised. But then my insecurities started. Maybe he just meant at work. Maybe he was trying to send me a message that he didn't want to be romantically involved anymore. "You sure you really believe that?"

"Don't you?"

"I don't know what I think." I felt muddled and apprehensive, all because of a fucking Post-it note on the damn coffee maker.

He didn't speak. He merely frowned and stared straight ahead.

The moment was ripe for a heart-to-heart. He'd opened the door, and I could easily have started a conversation about *us*. If I were anyone but the insecure mess I seemed to be, I would probably have asked him flat out how he felt about me romantically. I knew I should clear the air, face whatever he had to say head-on. After all, maybe comfort and good things awaited me. Maybe he'd tell me everything I wanted to hear — that he still loved me and that the future still didn't look right without me in it. My heart pounded as I tried to summon the courage to be a grown-up and have a grown-up conversation. I opened my mouth to speak, and his phone buzzed. I snapped my mouth closed as he answered his cell.

I knew immediately that he was talking to someone close to him. The gentle timbre of his voice was different than when he spoke to coworkers. He didn't say a name though, and I had no idea if he was talking to a man or a woman.

Thompson isn't the kind of man who cheats.

No. Thompson would never cheat. I swallowed hard. He'd be up-front. Maybe he'd try and talk it out first, let me down easy. Maybe he'd start the withdrawing process by spending less time at my place and leaving notes on coffee makers.

I clenched my jaw and listened to his conversation. He was making dinner plans for tonight. My stomach tensed, and I tried to appear unconcerned. But my nails dug into my palms as I plastered a fake pleasant expression on. He hung up and I stared out the window, my pulse zipping along like a heart attack victim's.

He cleared his throat. "Do you have plans tonight?"

Surprised at his question, I slid my gaze to his. "No."

"Well, my brother Jeff is in town." He sounded stiff.

Jeff was his younger brother. "You mean the one who set you up on that blind date a few months back?"

He laughed awkwardly. "The one and the same."

I waited for him to continue.

"He called me yesterday, and he wants to have dinner tonight." He slowed down and turned into the parking lot at the station. "I was going to just meet him alone... but maybe you'd like to come with?"

Keeping my face blank, I said, "So then you don't have a lot of stuff to catch up on after all?"

He frowned. "I'm sorry?"

"The note you left this morning, it said you were sleeping at your place tonight because you had stuff to catch up on."

He pulled into a parking spot and turned off the engine. He glanced over. "Yeah, um… I wasn't sure if you meeting my family was a good idea."

"Why not?"

He shrugged. "It seems like something you only do if you're super serious with someone."

I didn't know how to take that. We'd said we loved each other—was that not serious enough? "But you changed your mind?"

He pinched the skin between his eyes. "I originally was going to have you meet Jeff tonight."

I frowned. "I'm seriously lost."

He grimaced. "My original plan was to have you two meet. But then I changed my mind because something made me question… us."

My stomach sank. "You're questioning us?" I felt numb as his words sank in. So I'd been right. He had been acting weird.

He glanced around the parking lot. "This isn't really the time or the place."

I scowled and shifted to face him. "Too fucking bad. You need to tell me what's going on in that head of yours." I pinned him with my frustrated gaze. "If you don't want to be with me, just say so."

"I didn't say that. And I wouldn't introduce you to my brother if I didn't see a future with you." He sighed. "Or at least I did. *Fuck*. I'm confused."

"Jesus, Thompson, just tell me what the hell is going on."

He dropped his gaze to the dashboard. "Remember I said you talk in your sleep?"

"Yes."

"Well, you said something last night, and it got to me." He winced. "It made me start wondering if I'm maybe just a stand-in, or I was just there when you needed comfort."

"Wait. What?"

"From losing Will. It made me wonder if maybe being with me is simply better than being alone." His voice was hushed. "Because if that's what I am to you, I don't want that."

"That's not what this is." I felt breathless.

He gave a hard laugh. "I hoped it wasn't, but from the beginning, there was always a tiny doubt at the back of my mind. But I pushed it away because I wanted to be with you." He swallowed hard. "Then something you said last night kind of brought it back."

Wrinkling my brow, I asked, "What did I say?"

"It was like you were talking to Will in the dream," he murmured, instead of answering me.

"Thompson, what the heck did I say?"

He winced. "That you'd never loved anybody but Will, and that you never would."

Chapter Four

My stomach clenched at how hurt he sounded. "That's not true. You must know that isn't true."

He avoided my gaze. "I don't know, Liam. I think maybe it is."

"Seriously?"

"I heard you very clearly."

"How can you blame me for the rambling shit I might say when I'm sound asleep?" I touched his arm, and he stiffened. "Come on, Thompson. You're not like this. You're not insecure or jealous."

He gave a harsh laugh. "I am with you, Liam. And I hate it."

My heart banged against my ribs. "You don't need to be. You know how I feel about you."

"I thought I did."

"Wow." I stared straight ahead, feeling numb.

"I told you we shouldn't get into this."

"Yeah." I grimaced. "But I thought we'd simply talk about whatever silly thing was bothering you. But if you really think I just used you so I didn't have to be alone... I'm not sure what to say."

"I'm not saying you did it consciously."

I huffed. "No? Gee, thanks."

"Liam—"

"So your theory is I'm so weak-minded, I just go with the flow? I'll just bang anyone who's around so I'm not alone?" I shook my head. "Do you not hear how insulting that is?"

"I'm not saying that. I'm saying you sought comfort and… you know… I was familiar."

I wasn't sure if I was mad or hurt. Maybe I was both. I grabbed the door handle. "You were right. We shouldn't talk about this right now." I got out of the car.

He got out too, and he led the way up the walkway to the front of the station. Before we went in, he stopped and turned to me. "Don't be mad."

I shrugged, not sure how to respond.

"You told me to talk, and now you're mad."

"That's because I thought maybe you'd say something like you didn't like how I hogged the covers, or used the last of the half-and-half. I didn't expect you to tell me I'm a heartless asshole who used my friend because I'm so pathetic I can't be alone."

"Well, when you say it out loud, it sounds really bad."

I rolled my eyes and pushed past him to go in the building. The elevator was empty and once inside, he turned to me, anxiety clearly written on his face. "I'm not an expert on relationships. You know that. I'm trying to find my way."

I frowned. "How do I know that you're not just making all this up because you really don't want to be in a relationship?"

"What? That's silly."

"Is it? I don't think so. You've avoided anything serious with people for most of your adult life. Maybe you're a commitmentphobe."

Scowling, he said. "Right. A commitmentphobe who wants you to meet my family."

Point one to Thompson.

"Yeah, but that hasn't happened yet. All you've done is talk about it. And on the day when your brother is actually available, suddenly you have a big problem with me." I watched him through narrowed eyes. "How very convenient."

He laughed, which was the last thing I expected.

"You think it's funny?"

"No." He grimaced and moved closer. "I think… I think that we're both so fucking scared of what this is we're acting stupid."

I studied him in silence for a moment. "Okay… I can admit I'm scared."

"Me too. And I know I'm acting stupid because of that, Liam. But I don't want to lose you." He moved to put his hand behind my neck, pulling me in for a kiss. His warm lips covered mine, and I melted into him, winding my arms around his narrow waist.

It felt so good to have him against me, it made me feel like we were a unit again. I sighed when he lifted his head, and we smiled hesitantly at each other. "I've been confused all day. Confused and worried."

"Me too." His voice was husky.

I fingered his collar, keeping my eyes on a button on his shirt. "My feelings haven't changed for you, Thompson. Not at all."

"Are you sure?" he asked gruffly.

"God. Yes." I sighed.

"Mine neither."

"Then maybe we should relax and stop scrutinizing every little thing. I know I've been doing that. If you're ten minutes late to my place, I assume you've met someone new."

He gave a short laugh. "All I do is examine every word and gesture. It's exhausting, and it's not conducive to happiness."

"No. Take it from a professional neurotic, it's a bad thing."

"The two-month mark is usually when I lose interest." His eyes were searching. "But that isn't the case with you. I still want this."

I exhaled with relief. "Well, you have me."

"Okay."

I frowned and said, "But please don't hold me responsible for the nonsense I might babble when I'm asleep. I have no idea what goes on in my dreams."

"Maybe I'll get you a muzzle."

"Very funny." I pulled away from him as the elevator dinged. I felt as if a weight had been lifted from my chest as we moved toward the interview rooms. I sneaked a peek at Thompson's handsome profile, thankful he'd let his guard down enough to make things right. At least for now.

A uniformed officer approached. "You've got four kids waiting. They all seem willing to talk and pretty damn freaked-out."

"Can you blame them?" Thompson said, taking some papers from the officer.

The cop shook his head and continued past us. We made our way to the first room, and when we opened it, a Hispanic girl sat there under the flickering fluorescent lights. Her eyes were puffy and her face pale. She straightened as we closed the door and sat across from her.

"Hello... Grace." Thompson read her name off the sheet he held. "I'm Detective Thompson, and this is Liam Baker."

"Hi," she said softly.

Her brown eyes were filled with worry, and she started chewing on her cuticles as Thompson shuffled some papers. "So it says here you knew Gloria from the psychology class you had together?"

She nodded. "Yes. But we were close before that. We've known each other since high school."

"I see." Thompson nodded. "Did you see Gloria last night?"

She frowned. "Well, yeah, we had our class."

"Okay. How did she seem?"

"Fine." She was a little hard to read at first because she kept her emotions bottled up well. But I was able to worm my way into her mind eventually. This wasn't the first time she'd been interviewed by police. She'd been busted for shoplifting a few times in the past. But she certainly wasn't a criminal mastermind; she was just a kid who'd wanted pink nail polish but hadn't had the money.

"She didn't seem upset about anything at all?" Thompson's tone was pleasant and almost conversational.

Shrugging, Grace said, "If she was upset, she didn't share that with me."

"But you two were friends?" I asked, sweeping her mind and finding multiple instances of her and Gloria whispering and sharing a laugh.

"Yes. We... we were friends." Her eyes seemed to tear up, and she sniffed. "I can't believe she's dead."

"It must be a horrible shock." Thompson gave her a sympathetic look.

"It is. She was such a good person. Why would anyone want to hurt her?"

Thompson sat back in his chair. "It's hard to say why people do things."

She dropped her gaze to the table top. "Yeah."

"Were Gloria and Kyle having problems?" I asked. I purposely wanted to jar her a little. She was hiding something, and I wanted to know what. If you really wanted your friend's killer to be caught, you shouldn't be hiding shit from the cops.

She swallowed hard. "Is that what he told you?"

"He? You mean Kyle?" I asked.

"Yeah."

"We're asking you the question. It doesn't matter what Kyle did or didn't tell us." Thompson watched her closely.

She licked her lips and looked around. "Kyle wouldn't hurt her. If that's what you mean."

"You didn't answer the question," Thompson nudged.

"Relationships are hard." Her voice wobbled.

"So is that a yes? She and Kyle were having problems?" Thompson asked.

"They were two really different people. They met when they were so young, and people change. I think it was starting to interfere with how they felt about each other."

"In what way?" Thompson crossed his hands on the table.

"You know... they were growing apart."

"Okay." Thompson nodded, scribbling some notes.

The jarring image of Grace and Kyle fucking slammed into my brain, causing me to grunt. Thompson glanced over at me with a questioning look. I cleared my throat and addressed her. "Would you say you were closer to Kyle or Gloria?"

Her face turned pink. "Both."

"Come on, Grace," I coaxed. "Which one of them were you closer to lately?"

She crossed her arms. "Kyle would never hurt her. That's all I know."

"We never said he would."

"Yeah, but I know how you cops are. You always think it's the boyfriend." She clenched her jaw. "Kyle's not violent."

"So you saw Gloria during your psychology class." Thompson changed the subject abruptly, and she grimaced. "When it ended, did you see where she went? Because she wasn't attacked anywhere near her psych class or the parking lot her car was in."

"We went our separate ways after class."

"But you knew what she was doing after class, didn't you?" I was able to read her now. She'd known where Gloria was without a doubt. She'd walked with her friend to the gymnasium. Why was she lying? I didn't get the sense that she was actually involved in Gloria's murder. Was it simply guilt for sleeping with her best friend's boyfriend?

"Shouldn't I have a lawyer?" Her shame was palpable.

"No. We're just asking a few questions. You're not under arrest." Thompson's voice was reassuring.

"Still." She bit her lip, her guilt over cheating with Kyle now coming off her in waves.

"Grace, we don't care that you and Kyle are seeing each other." I leaned toward her.

She gasped and her lower lip quivered. "No we aren't."

"Yes. You are."

"How would you know that?" Her face was pink, and she looked rattled.

I put my finger to my temple. "I'm a psychic."

"Very funny."

"He's not kidding," Thompson murmured.

Her eyes widened as she stared at me. "What? Why would you be here?"

"Liam freelances with us on tricky cases," Thompson said.

She continued to stare at me like I was Bigfoot.

I held her gaze unflinchingly. "We don't care about what you and Kyle were up to. We just want details about Gloria's last night on earth."

She winced. "I don't know anything. Not really."

"You're lying," I said gruffly. "Why won't you help us catch your friend's killer?"

Her face crumpled, and she started sniffling. She wiped at her eyes roughly, giving little sobs every now and then. "You think I know more than I do. She didn't tell me anything, not really. She was being super secretive about the guy."

Bingo.

"So there was another guy." Thompson scribbled on his notepad. "You're sure you don't have even a first name?"

"No." She sighed. "I'm pretty sure she didn't want to tell me because she was afraid it would get back to the others."

"What others?" I frowned. "You mean Kyle?"

"Well, him too. But no, I mean the group." She wiped her eyes. "You know, that suicide club."

Thompson leaned toward her, his eyes focused like a laser. "Sure, we know about that. Can you refresh my memory on who runs that group?"

"Percy Johnson started it." She shrugged.

"Why would her private life be of concern to that group?" I asked.

"They're all pretty close in there. You know, they share a lot of personal stuff with each other. I don't think Percy likes people hooking up in the group. He says it causes unnecessary drama. But Gloria met some guy in there, and they really hit it off. They kept their feelings super-secret so Percy wouldn't get bent out of shape. She wouldn't even spill his name to me. It kind of pissed me off to be honest. I mean, when you won't even tell your best friend your secrets, that's fucked-up."

About as fucked-up as sleeping with your best friend's boyfriend.

"Yeah. That's a drag," I said, trying hard not to roll my eyes.

"Do you happen to have Percy's phone number?" Thompson asked.

"No." She sounded almost insulted. "God. I didn't belong to that club."

"So you walked with Gloria to where she was meeting her new friend." I glanced at Thompson. "But then you just parted ways?"

She nodded. "She went into the gym, and I took off because I wanted to see if maybe I could meet up with Kyle, since Gloria was… busy." Her cheeks tinted pink. "But when I called him, he was so high I didn't bother. I just went home."

"And the last time you saw or spoke to Gloria was outside the gym?" Thompson asked.

"Yes. But like I said, I didn't go inside. I called Kyle, but he was wasted, so I got in my car and drove home." Her mouth drooped. "I can't believe anyone would do that to her. She was so kindhearted. I mean, she and Kyle had problems because she wanted more and he's immature." She scowled. "Obviously he's immature since he gets high, like, constantly."

"But you still like him," I said. She was completely smitten; it was easy to read.

"Yes. He has his good side."

"Why would Gloria want more with Kyle if she was into this other guy?" I asked.

She shrugged. "I think she'd stopped pushing for more with Kyle a while ago. She was catching on that he wasn't ready for a real commitment. And at first, I thought maybe she was just seeing the new guy to make Kyle jealous. But since she kept it secret, that wasn't it. You can't make someone jealous if they don't know about the other person."

"Hmmm." I frowned. "She must have really liked this other dude."

"Do you think he's the one who killed her?" Grace's voice was hushed.

"We don't know." Thompson gathered his papers as he spoke. "We appreciate you talking with us, Grace. It might just help us find the person who killed Gloria." Thompson stood, his chair scraping on the tile floor.

She got up slowly, hanging her head. "You won't tell anyone about... about Kyle and me, right?"

"No. Like Liam said, that's not our focus."

"Okay." She left the room looking demoralized.

I met Thompson's dark gaze. "At least we have the name of the group leader."

"Yep. Maybe we can go have a little chat with him after we finish with these other kids."

"Someone in that group might know her secret guy's name."

"If she didn't tell Grace, I doubt it."

"Good point." I followed him out of the room.

The next three students knew even less about Gloria's personal life than Grace had. Since we weren't really getting any good information, we cut the interviews short and figured the person to talk to was Percy Johnson. We knew he'd had several classes during the day, but it was after three by the time we were free. We decided to go to his house and interview him there, instead of dragging him to the police precinct. Sometimes people were more relaxed when you spoke to them away from the station. It felt more informal to them, and so they were more open.

We drove to the address we had on file for him. When he opened the door and we introduced ourselves, he didn't look that surprised to see us. Most people were definitely nervous when the cops showed up, but Percy almost seemed like he'd been expecting us.

He invited us in, and we sat across from him on a tattered brown sofa. The first thing that struck me about Percy was that he had red hair, and his build was similar to the killer's. However, the odds of finding Gloria's killer this easily seemed unlikely. It also worked in his favor that he seemed very open and willing to help.

"I was horrified to hear about Gloria." His eyes were warm and concerned. "She was a wonderful person."

"How long was she a member of your Always Listening group?" Thompson asked.

"Oh, she joined up almost at the beginning." He swallowed hard. "It was only four of us at the start, and we all really bonded. Of course, now there are twenty people in the group. Suicidal thoughts and depression are far more prevalent than you might think."

"Did Gloria seem unusually close to anyone in the club?" Thompson's gaze was keen.

"She and Tim really hit it off. He was one of the originals like us."

"Do you have Tim's full name?" Thompson sounded casual.

"Of course. Hernandez is his last name." He scrunched his face. "She was also good friends with Lucy Bilden and Anthony Murphy."

I tried to dig deeper into his brain, but he wasn't easy to read. He had a lot of surface thoughts but nothing that was terribly meaty. I wasn't sure if that was because there wasn't anything to find or if he was good at hiding his thoughts. But Thompson hadn't introduced me as a psychic, so I had no reason to think he was deliberately hiding anything.

"When was the last time you saw Gloria?" Thompson asked.

"Monday night. That's when Always Listening meets." He sighed. "She seemed in great spirits."

"Were you on campus last night?" Thompson leaned back and crossed his legs, giving off a nonchalant vibe.

Percy nodded. "Yes. I had two classes."

"Did you happen to see Gloria? Even briefly?" I asked.

He frowned. "No. Not last night. I had a calculus test, and I was pretty focused on that. I also had medieval literature, but I barely remember being in that class, I was so consumed with what I had to do."

"What you had to do?" I lifted one brow.

Percy frowned. "Yeah. You know... pass my test."

"Awww. Right." I smiled politely. His mannerisms were odd, but I didn't get a violent feeling from him. It was hard to imagine this mild-mannered, almost foppish guy strangling Gloria with a belt. Also, Gloria had looked infatuated in the vision I'd had of her in the gym. Percy didn't seem the type to make girls swoon. "What time did your math class end?"

"I finished the test at ten forty-five, and I came straight home."

"Do you have a roommate? Anyone who can verify you were here?" Thompson glanced around the living room, honing in on the fireplace mantel where there were photos of Percy with an older woman.

"I live with my mom." His face tensed as if he was embarrassed to admit his living situation. "She's not well. I try and help out by being here."

"That's good of you," I offered. "Did she see you last night when you got home?"

"We had a brief conversation."

"Is she here now?" Thompson asked.

"Yes. But she's asleep."

I nodded. "Maybe we can talk to her another day?"

"Sure. When she's up to it."

"We have to verify your whereabouts. Nothing personal. It's just something we'd do with anyone," I added softly.

"Of course. I understand."

"I assume you talk about very personal stuff in your group." Thompson asked, changing the subject.

"Extremely. We're a suicide support group, so that kind of goes without saying."

"And Gloria confided in you about her suicide attempt?" I watched him closely.

He hung his head. "Yes. And I confided my attempt too."

"So you didn't just start the group to help others, but you also needed that support?" Thompson's tone was emotionless.

Glancing up, Percy's eyes were bright. "When you decide to end your life, it's an earth-shattering experience. No one can understand like another person who's gone through it. It's nice to talk to people who get it. They don't ask the same stupid questions as people who haven't."

"I can see that." I met Thompson's gaze, feeling self-conscious since I'd tried to take my life after losing William. If not for Thompson, I wouldn't have been alive today.

"Can you?" Percy seemed to perk up as he watched me. "Do I sense a kindred spirit?"

My face warmed at how astute he was, but I kept my expression blank and didn't respond. We weren't here to talk about me.

Clearing his throat, Thompson rose. "Do you have the phone numbers or addresses for the other members in the club?"

Thankful he'd interrupted Percy's line of questioning, I got to my feet too.

Percy hesitated, his gaze still trained on me. "I have everybody's info."

"We'll need that," Thompson said.

Percy pulled his cell from his pocket. "Would you like me to write it down now, or should I send it to you through email?"

Thompson pursed his lips. "How about you write down Tim, Lucy, and Anthony's info now. Then go ahead and email me the rest of the group's contact info."

"Sure." Percy moved to a desk nearby. He sat and wrote on a pad for a few minutes, then stood and handed the paper to Thompson. "Um... do you have any good leads yet?" he asked, biting his lip. "I hate to think this person could get away with killing Gloria."

"It's way too soon to really know anything." Thompson was evasive.

Percy nodded. "Right. That, and you probably wouldn't tell me anyway." His laugh was stiff. "I suppose we're all suspects."

"Unfortunately, anyone Gloria knew has to come under scrutiny." I hoped I sounded empathetic. I did feel sympathy for him. It would be horrible to lose a friend and also be suspected of taking their life. But since it was usually someone the victim knew, we had to interview everyone we could.

"I suppose so." Percy sighed. "But just FYI, I can't even kill spiders."

I smiled. "We'll keep that in mind."

Thompson moved to the door and held up the slip of paper Percy had given him. "Thanks for the info."

"Of course. I hope I was helpful." Percy rested his hands on his hips.

That movement made me glance down to his belt, and a chill went through me as I recognized it as the identical belt the killer had used to strangle Gloria.

S.C. Wynne

Chapter Five

I hoped my face gave nothing away as we left his house. But my heart pounded as we slid into the car. Thompson started the engine, and I put my hand on his arm.

He turned to look at me, and he frowned. "What is it?"

"Did you happen to notice his belt?"

"No." He narrowed his eyes. "Why?"

"It was exactly the same style as the one wrapped around Gloria's neck." The image of that belt cutting into her white throat made my stomach roll.

"Are you sure?"

"Yes. I remember it was distinctive in that there was a line of stitching that ran down the center of the belt." I swallowed. "And the tip was silver. It stood out to me."

He bit his bottom lip. "We should be able to find out the make of that belt to see if it's an unusual style or not."

"Okay." I felt breathless.

"It might be super common."

"Maybe."

"We can't arrest him based just on his belt." Thompson rubbed his jaw. "We need to place him near the scene at the time of death or establish a more intimate relationship with the victim."

"I know. But he has red hair, and he's the same build as the guy I saw strangling Gloria. Doesn't that all seem like a lot of coincidence?"

"Definitely. But we need more." Thompson pulled into traffic. "We need to talk to his mom ASAP. If he's lying about when he got home, that would be good to know."

I wrinkled my brow. "As much as his belt weirds me out, I really didn't get any sense of him being a violent guy. He's a bit strange, but he didn't give off any bad vibrations. Although, his brain wasn't easy to get into either."

"You mean like he was hiding something?"

"We're all hiding things all the time, so that doesn't necessarily make him a murderer. But he was really closed off at first. I got in, but it took a little work."

Thompson sighed. "It's early for forensics to have much for us yet." He sounded frustrated. "We need to bring in those three kids from the Always Listening club. Today if possible."

I held out my hand for the paper that Percy had given him with the club member's info. "You want me to call them and see if they can come in and talk to us later this afternoon?"

He dug in his jean's pocket. "Yes. I'd kill to talk to them right away."

"Interesting choice of words coming from a homicide detective."

He smirked and handed me the paper. "Don't make any appointments any later than four thirty. We have dinner reservations for six."

My stomach clenched. "With Jeff?"

"Yep." He glanced over and then returned his gaze to the road. "You still in?"

"Dinner with your brother makes me nervous. Not gonna lie." The Thompson clan was closely knit. That was intimidating to someone like me. My family had been the opposite of close. However, I knew me getting to know his family was important to Thompson, so I would have to suck it up. "I want this to work, and I'm a hundred percent in."

"Awww." He laughed gruffly. "That was sweet."

"Shut up."

"I'm serious. You rarely say anything that soft and gooey."

"If you keep mocking me, I won't ever say anything nice again."

His chuckle made my chest tighten with affection.

Glancing out the window at the grimy buildings we passed, my mind drifted back to the case. "Wouldn't it be amazing if somehow that belt led us to the killer in one day?"

"Unless we get a spontaneous confession, that isn't going to happen."

"I know. But it would be cool to solve this murder that quickly."

"I'd be a miracle."

"I would definitely buy a lotto ticket." I slid my gaze to his profile. "Plus it would put to rest this nagging feeling that Pine is somehow involved in this case."

His jaw tensed. "You should put that to rest regardless. He. Is. In. Jail."

"Yep."

His impatience seeped into me, but he didn't speak.

I probably should have dropped the subject because I knew it irritated him, but I wanted him to understand how real the connection to Pine felt to me. I wasn't just making these feelings up. "It's easier for you to dismiss him. You think in absolutes. But the psychic world is anything *but* that, and I've never met a stronger psychic than Pine. I have no idea what he's capable of."

"The strongest psychic in the world can't be physically in two places."

"Yes. I know that. And you're right, he can't be physically in two places. But remember how he hijacked the dead spirit's energy before? I'd never heard of that happening in real life. I'd heard the theory tossed around, but no one had ever done it until I met Pine. Not that I'm aware of anyway."

"Okay, but he's in jail. He couldn't have touched Gloria, so he couldn't hijack her energy." He laughed gruffly. "I can't believe what I'm even saying."

I scowled at him. "What does that mean?"

"Just that it's weird to actually accept that psychic stuff is real."

"You'd better think it's real." I studied his profile. "You've seen enough by now to know it's legit."

"Yes. I know you're legit. But it still feels weird to say things like someone hijacked a dead person's energy aloud. Most of my life I didn't believe in psychics."

The wall around his mind slipped a little, and I was able to peek inside his brain for a second. I got a glimpse of him being ribbed by that asshole Officer Perrell and a few of his nonbelieving pals.

Sighing, I muttered, "Plus your little cop buddies think you're romantically involved with a nutcase. I get it. It's hard to stand up for something you secretly still think is crazy." A part of me understood Thompson's dilemma. While the things he'd seen with me couldn't be denied, his logic still told him that was all impossible, that there had to be more reasonable explanations for all of the things we'd experienced.

"I can't blame them for not believing." He sounded defensive.

"I know. Hardly anyone does."

"Liam, you know I'm on your side. You know I know you're the real deal."

"Yep." I wasn't mad at him. He was doing the best he could to accept the things he saw. "It's just the way it is."

We fell silent. There was no point in beating a dead horse. He couldn't really tell me what I wanted to hear. Thompson couldn't help how he felt, and he was trying hard to be open-minded. Besides, compared to how he'd been when we'd first met, he was a true believer. He'd come around more and more as time passed. I was sure of it.

I called the kids from the group to arrange meetings later in the day. Lucy and Anthony were available, but Tim couldn't come in until the next day.

When we reached the station, we went to Thompson's desk to see if anything had been processed yet from the crime scene. He scrolled through his emails, and he perked up at one point. "They have the manufacturer of the belt already." He glanced at me, his eyes bright.

"Oh, good." I moved to stand over his shoulder as he scrolled. "That was fast."

"I may or may not have bribed Kevin from forensics with Lakers tickets."

"Nice."

He squinted at the computer screen. "The belt, AKA murder weapon, is made by a Detroit company named Shinola. Looks like the company sells stuff online directly, and also Nordstrom carries their stuff."

"Nordstrom?" I sighed. "God, they just had a huge sale this last weekend. Like fifty percent off everything in the store."

He frowned at me. "Did you want to talk about shopping?"

I rolled my eyes. "Yeah, and then later we can talk about my skin care routine. I've been using a vitamin C serum that's the bomb."

He grinned at my sardonic tone.

"My point is, if the local stores carry that belt, it's probable they sold a bunch of them last weekend."

"I'll get Tracy to call the local Nordstrom's and see how many of these exact belts they sold." He frowned. "Forensics didn't find any prints on the belt."

"Not surprising. The killer had on gloves, remember?"

"Yep. But sometime crooks are sloppy." He leaned back in his chair. "Unless we can connect Percy to the belt used to kill Gloria though, all we have is a guy who likes the same style belt as the killer."

"Probably a popular style too. It was a nice belt."

His lips twitched. "Now I know what to get you for your birthday."

I shuddered. "Please don't."

He sighed. "At the moment Percy's belt is nothing more than coincidence. But we still need to keep our eyes on the kid."

"Definitely."

One of the other detectives walked up. "A Lucy Bilden is here to see you?"

"Could you put her in interview room C?" Thompson asked.

"Sure thing." The detective walked away whistling.

Thompson stood and pulled on his jacket. I let my gaze linger on his wide shoulders, trailing down over his flat stomach while enjoying the view. Two months of seeing each other almost every night, and I still couldn't seem to get enough of the guy.

Our eyes met, and he winked. "Looking forward to dinner tonight?"

I grimaced. "Not really."

"Why not?" He frowned and led the way to the interview room.

"Because what if Jeff doesn't like me?" Thompson wasn't a pushover, and I couldn't really see him dumping me just because his brother didn't love me. But if Jeff disliked me, he might color the rest of the family's opinion of me. He probably already hated me because I'd fucked up his buddy Denny's romance with Thompson.

"He'll love you."

"Yeah, right. I'm not everybody's cup of tea."

He knocked my elbow with his. "I kind of like you. Isn't that all that matters?"

I laughed. "I guess."

We entered the interview room and found a wispy blonde girl. Her eyes were wide, and she looked uneasy. "Why am I here?" Her voice wobbled.

"Well, as I explained on the phone, you were good friends with Gloria and we're trying to find out as much as we can about her last day." I smiled at her, trying to put her at ease. She was hugely nervous and upset over her friend's death. From reading her compassionate energy, I doubted she had any connection to Gloria's murder, but she might still have information that could prove useful.

Thompson sat across from her, and I sat next to him. As I opened my senses to her, it became clear she was like reading a picture book. She'd adored Gloria and wouldn't hurt a fly. She volunteered at an elderly home after school most days and worked at a homeless shelter as well. If she'd had anything to do with Gloria's murder, I'd eat my shoe.

Her gaze was warm as she answered questions from Thompson. And when we moved on to discussing the actual murder, she went so white I was afraid she'd keel over.

"Oh, God. I can't even bear to think about that. She must have been so scared." She gave a whimper.

"She fought hard." My voice was hushed.

"But it didn't do any good." She sniffed, dabbing at her eyes with her fingers. "Sorry. I'm feeling so emotional."

"No need to apologize." I pushed a box of tissues toward her, and she smiled at me in thanks. "Is there any chance you knew the name of her new boyfriend?" I asked.

She dropped her gaze, and her candid energy changed. "You mean Kyle?" It wasn't really in her nature to be evasive, and she looked uncomfortable as she glanced everywhere in the room but at us.

"Come on, Lucy. You know we don't mean Kyle," I nudged.

She sighed. "Yeah. I know. I just don't want you thinking poorly of her."

"You mean because she was seeing someone on the side besides Kyle?"

"Yes," she whispered.

"We're here to solve her murder, Lucy. Not to judge her." Thompson's voice was sincere.

"Okay." She glanced up, smiling weakly.

"So, who was this mysterious guy? Why doesn't anyone know anything about him?" Thompson tapped his pen on the table distractedly.

"Gloria was super clammed up about him. At first, I thought it was because she didn't want Kyle to find out." She frowned. "But then she told me that the guy didn't want her to tell anyone. He wanted their relationship to be a secret."

"But why?" Thompson scowled. "What's the big deal if they liked each other? She easily could have broken it off with Kyle and dated this guy openly."

"I know. I said the same thing to her. Maybe he got off on the secrecy of it. Or maybe he had a girlfriend. I don't know."

"And you never caught a glimpse of him?" I asked.

She shook her head. "No. I only knew about him because they had a little spat, and she needed someone to talk to."

"What kind of spat?" Thompson asked.

"It's kind of embarrassing to talk about." Her cheeks were flushed.

"It could be important, Lucy," Thompson coaxed.

She winced. "It's sexual in nature."

"You can't shock us. We've heard it all." He met my gaze, and I nodded.

She bit her lip, looking pained. "God. Okay. She said that they only slept together twice." She dropped her gaze. "But that the second time… the second time he put his hands around her throat and almost choked her out during it." She shivered, looking up with repulsion written clearly on her face. "Isn't that disgusting?"

I widened my eyes. "He tried to choke her during… sex?"

She nodded.

"And she still kept seeing him?"

"I know. That would be it for me if a guy did that." She scrunched her face in distaste.

"Was that her only problem with him?" Thompson asked.

I frowned. "Isn't that enough?"

He ignored me. "Did they seem to get along usually?"

"Well… she said he'd been acting really moody — not like himself at all. And then he did that, and she was freaked-out." She sighed. "But they worked it out, I guess, because she never brought it up again." She hung her head. "That was two weeks ago… and now she's dead."

"How about a name? Did she maybe use a name?" Thompson leaned toward her, keeping his voice even.

"I don't know his real name, but she called him Clinky."

I pulled my brows together. "Why?"

"She said he wore a necklace around his neck that made a clinking sound." She sighed. "God, I feel sick just thinking about all of this."

"Was... Clinky... in a class with her?" Thompson asked.

"She wouldn't say."

I could sense Thompson's frustration. We were getting nowhere today. Lucy had given us a lot of information, but it wasn't the kind we could use to track the killer down. We couldn't exactly put out an APB on a person named "Clinky." The sad part was that Gloria had successfully blocked all her friends out of this part of her life, and now that made solving her murder difficult.

We spent another ten minutes with Lucy, hoping she'd give us something more concrete, but she didn't know anything else. By the time she left, Anthony Murphy had arrived to talk to us. When we entered the room where he waited and saw he was a redhead, me and Thompson shared a look. He was the same build as the killer, just as Percy had been. I'd never met so many gingers in one day, and I was beginning to feel like the universe was mocking me.

"Thanks for coming in, Anthony," Thompson greeted the nervous-looking kid.

"My pleasure." He winced. "Well, not really a pleasure, but you know what I mean."

I got a sense of him immediately. He was brokenhearted over Gloria's death. They'd been extremely close, and he'd had a crush on her. But he'd hidden it from her and everybody else. "We're trying to find out any information we can about a guy Gloria was seeing."

He kept his gaze down. "Yeah. She had the hots for some random guy." He flicked his gaze to Thompson's. "Not Kyle."

"Exactly. But no one has any info on this mystery man." Thompson studied Anthony.

"Did Gloria tell you about this new guy?"

Anthony scowled. "She didn't tell me. I overheard her talking with Lucy, and I had to drag it out of her. He sounded sketchy as fuck to me. He told her not to tell anyone about them, or he'd break up with her. I mean, what a dick. Who says that to a girl?" His eyes were full of pain. "She deserved so much better."

"Would you happen to know his name?" Thompson asked half-heartedly, as if fully expecting a negative answer.

"No."

Figures.

"All I know is they met here at school, and he was very controlling. He told her what to wear, and he wouldn't let her color her hair. He said it would make her less pure." Anthony curled his lip. "That's some insecure shit right there."

"He wouldn't let her color her hair?" I frowned.

"Nope. He had her fasting too. She almost fainted a bunch of times because he insisted she only drink water for two days straight."

"Why would she go along with that?" I asked.

"Because she was in love with the guy. She'd have done anything for him, I think." Anthony slumped. "He told her they were destined to meet and that it was written in the stars or some nonsense. She believed him."

"Was Gloria a gullible girl usually?" Thompson asked.

"That's just it... no. Not at all. But this guy wormed his way into her heart, and she just obeyed him blindly."

"Everybody we've talked to says they never saw the guy. It's hard to believe no one saw them together." Thompson's gaze was doubtful. "Not even a tiny glimpse."

Anthony's face tensed, and I suddenly had a vision of him lurking around the exterior of the gymnasium. In the vision he was angry, and his jealousy radiated from him as he watched through a crack in the back door of the building.

"Anthony." My voice was hard. "You saw him."

Widening his eyes, he shook his head. "No I didn't."

"You did. I know you did." I leaned toward him. "I know you're embarrassed because you spied on Gloria. But anything you saw, you need to tell us."

Red spears of color appeared on his cheeks. "You're crazy."

Thompson exhaled impatiently. "I neglected to mention that Liam here is a psychic, Anthony. There's no point in lying because he knows what's going on inside your head."

Anthony looked mortified. "Shut the fuck up."

"It's true. I already know you followed Gloria. Now we just need to know what or who you saw."

"I don't believe you."

I sighed. "Think of a number."

"What?" He pulled his brows tight.

"Think of a number, and I'll guess what it is." I wasn't always good at this little parlor trick, but I could get into Anthony's mind really easily, so I wasn't worried.

He smirked. "Fine."

I probed his mind. "Ten."

Bugging his eyes, he looked at Thompson. "How did he do that?"

"I told you, he's a psychic."

"What letter am I thinking of?" Anthony asked, a stubborn set to his jaw.

"R."

"How about now?"

"Z."

"How about now?"

"That's not a letter... but eight."

His mouth dropped open. "Jesus. You're seriously a psychic?"

I nodded.

"All right. I followed her last night."

"I know." I sighed. "What did you see?"

He slumped, and his face screwed up as if he was trying not to show his emotions. "I just wanted to protect her, you know? I knew the guy was bad news, and I just wanted to keep her safe." He looked up, his eyes haunted. "But I failed. And now she's dead."

"That's why you need to tell us everything you know," Thompson said quietly. "Any small detail could make the difference."

He grimaced. "The problem is I didn't really get a good look at the guy. He had on a hoodie, and he had his back to me." He rubbed his face roughly. "Not to mention when they started kissing, I almost puked. I had to get out of there."

"Did you ever follow her another time?"

"Yeah. Monday. Right after group."

"You mean after your Always Listening group?" Thompson asked, his eyes glittering as he watched Anthony.

"Yeah." He sighed. "I followed her after group, but I got hung up talking to a kid I knew from another class. By the time I got to the gym, the guy was already there with her. I wished I'd seen him walk in. Then I'd be able to tell you what he looked like."

"Hair color?"

"He had on a knit cap." Anthony shook his head.

Thompson sat back, his frustration obvious. "Yeah. That's really too bad."

"So you followed her two times, and both times you couldn't see his face?" I asked.

"Yes. If I didn't know better, I'd say the prick was purposely hiding what he looked like."

"Did his outline or mannerisms seem familiar in any way?" I asked. Anthony was the only person to have actually seen the killer, besides me. He knew Gloria's friends, whereas I didn't. It was entirely possible he knew the killer and went to classes with him. He might be able to pick up on personal details I wouldn't know.

"Not really. But like I said, I didn't stay long either time because it upset me too much when they started swapping spit."

"So you took off." Thompson wrote on his pad.

"Yeah."

Thompson put his pen down and leaned on his elbows, giving Anthony a stern look. "If you think of anything else, promise me you'll call us."

Shrugging, Anthony said, "Sure."

"It's entirely possible the killer is someone you know." I watched Anthony as I spoke.

He shivered. "That's hard to believe. I can't think of anyone I know who'd hurt Gloria."

"Someone close to her, who she trusted, choked the life from her." Thompson's mouth was a grim line. "So you need to keep your ears and eyes open, Anthony."

He touched his throat. "Jesus. Way to scare the shit out of a guy."

"We just want you on your guard." Thompson rose.

Anthony left the interview room, and Thompson turned to me, looking demoralized. The sad droop of his mouth ate at me. Of the two of us, he was generally more upbeat about the cases we worked than me. I hated seeing him down, and since we were alone in the room, I moved closer to him.

"It's almost four thirty. Ready to go eat some food and watch your boyfriend embarrass himself in front of your brother?" As I spoke, I slid my arms around him and then kissed him softly.

He responded, pulling me closer. After working my mouth with his tongue for a few moments, he lifted his head. "You're the one bright spot in my day." His voice was husky.

"Awww. Now you're the soft and gooey one."

He grinned. "Let's go. I need a shower."

"Why?" I inhaled in an exaggerated fashion. "I love the rough, masculine smell of you after a long day's work, Detective Thompson."

He chuckled and opened the door for me. "Do you mind if I shower at your place?"

"Sure. It'll save time."

"Not really. I was thinking we could shower together."

My pulse quickened. "You know if we're late, that won't endear me to your brother."

He licked his lips, his eyes glittering. "He's probably not going to like you anyway because of the whole Denny thing."

I scowled. "I thought you said he'd love me?"

His dimples appeared. "I lied."

Chapter Six

Jeff Thompson looked a lot like his older brother, only he was a little shorter, and he had a more open energy. I'd seen a picture of Jeff, but in person the resemblance was stronger. He was already seated when we arrived at the restaurant. When he saw us, he stood and held out his hand. He was much easier to read than his brother, and his thoughts made it clear he wasn't sure what to make of me.

Thompson ruffled his brother's hair, and his younger sibling looked a little annoyed. "Have you gotten even shorter?" Thompson grinned.

"Same jokes, different day." Jeff smirked, swatting his brother's hand away. He turned to me again. "So you're the famous Liam Baker."

I held his gaze, instinctively knowing that with a guy like him, acting meek would be a mistake. "Not sure what I'm famous for, but I'm Liam." His grip was like a vise, and I did my best not to wince.

"You accomplished the impossible." He slapped Thompson's back. "You got this old dog to settle down. That's quite an achievement." Jeff slid back into the booth.

"You love to exaggerate," Thompson muttered.

"Not really." Jeff laughed.

Thompson got in the booth first, and I followed. I was glad that I was across the table from Jeff; it gave me a little distance from his intense stare. I wasn't much of a drinker, but tonight I felt like I needed something. Between Jeff and the spirits of a bickering elderly couple who shared our booth, I'd rarely needed a drink more.

The waiter was prompt, and when I ordered a lemon drop martini, Thompson looked nonplussed. I was glad he hid his surprise though, and didn't shout out anything like, "Hey, lightweight, you usually don't drink!"

Jeff and Thompson both ordered draft beers, and once the waiter left, Thompson patted my leg under the table. I smiled at him, trying to ignore the fact that Jeff was staring at me intently. When I finally drummed up the nerve to meet Jeff's gaze, he didn't smile, just continued to watch me. I grimaced and wiped at my chin as a joke. "Do I have something on my face?"

He cracked a smile. "No. I'm just really curious about the man who finally made my playboy brother stop fucking around."

"Jeff," Thompson grumbled. "Come on."

"What? Am I wrong?" Jeff returned his gaze to mine. "But then he met you, and he's a changed man."

I shrugged. "We all have a past, right?"

"That is true."

Thompson studied his menu like it was the bible and he had a first communion test looming. I was able to read him just enough to ascertain that he didn't want to step in and protect me too much. He knew that wouldn't win his brother over, and he wanted to see if I could hold my own with Jeff. Hunching my shoulders and avoiding Jeff's piercing stare wouldn't win me points with this younger Thompson sibling. So I sucked in a breath and sat up straighter, hoping I was up to the challenge.

"You two met on the job?" Jeff asked.

"Yeah." I glanced at Thompson. "My late boyfriend convinced your brother to give me a chance helping on stubborn cases."

Jeff nodded. "Yeah, I heard about William. I'm sorry for your loss."

I grimaced. "Thanks."

"Losing William must have brought you two closer."

I smiled weakly. "It did. I was a little slow to realize I had feelings for your brother, but certain things happened that woke me up."

"You mean like me setting him up on a blind date with Denny?"

My face warmed at Jeff's sardonic tone. "Yep. I didn't love seeing him with anyone else. It forced me to take a chance."

"Glad I could help," Jeff said, twisting his lips. "Denny took it pretty hard though. He really liked you, bro."

Thompson winced. "I know. He was a good guy."

I hated talking or thinking about Denny. I was well aware Thompson and he had slept together, and it made my gut ache to think of Thompson with another man. My way of handling those feelings of jealousy was to pretend it hadn't happened. But if Jeff was going to keep bringing Denny up, my little game of sticking my head in the sand wasn't going to work.

Jeff eyed his silent brother. "Took you long enough to make your move on Liam. If I'd known you were interested in Liam, I'd never have set you up with Denny."

Thompson's jaw clenched, but he just shrugged.

"We thought of each other as friends," I said softly. "But that changed."

Jeff sighed. "Yep. I just feel guilty for getting Denny hurt."

Are we going to talk about Denny all night?

I exhaled, trying to ignore my churning gut and the mental images that wanted to enter my brain of Thompson fucking Denny. I realized that we were of an age where we'd both slept with other people, but it didn't mean I relished hearing about it.

Thompson seemed to pick up on my discomfort because he said firmly, "It was too late by the time Denny came around. I already had feelings for Liam by then."

"Well, I'm glad you found each other." Jeff smiled politely.

Liar.

"So, my brother tells me you're a psychic?" His tone was like most people's when they mentioned my "talent"—skeptical.

"Yep." The waiter arrived with our drinks, and it took enormous self-control not to grab my martini off his tray.

"That sounds fascinating." Jeff handed Thompson his beer and then took his own from the waiter. "Tell me about what you do."

I laughed, not because I felt amused but because I knew Jeff thought I was full of shit. I wasn't used to caring whether nonbelievers bought into my skills or not. But because Jeff was my lover's brother, I couldn't blow him off like I usually would. It was awkward.

"What's so funny?" Jeff sipped his drink, watching me over the rim.

"Nothing actually. It's just I can tell you don't believe in psychics."

Jeff lifted one brow. "Do most people?"

"Not really." True believers were few and far between. When strangers found out about my abilities, most people looked at me the way Jeff was doing now, like I was trying to sell them swamp land in Florida.

"Liam has helped solve a bunch of dead files since he came on board." Thompson stretched his leg out and rested his calf against mine. It was a subtle but reassuring gesture, and it helped soothe me. "He's the real deal."

"I never doubted him for a moment." Jeff smirked. "Well, maybe a bit."

"It's okay if you do. That's normal."

"Do you see the future?" Jeff asked.

Everybody seemed to think psychics only saw the future. It was a little annoying. "No. I mostly see past events. Generally, spirits reach out who feel they've been wronged. That's why working on murder cases suits my talents."

Wrinkling his brow, Jeff said, "So you see dead people? Like that Bruce Willis movie?"

"Pretty much."

"Are there some around us right now?" Jeff's expression was wary.

"Yes." I laughed and met Thompson's amused gaze. "We're sharing the booth with an elderly couple who are arguing about whether the wife's spaghetti sauce is better than this restaurant's. It's actually very distracting because this woman is really proud of her sauce, and the husband is being a little obtuse." I rubbed my temples.

Shuddering, Jeff squeaked, "You mean they're here at our table?"

"Spirits are everywhere. They won't bother you if you don't bother them."

Usually.

"Wow." He glanced at his brother. "And this doesn't freak you out?"

"I'm used to it."

"Can you read minds?"

"I can read some people's thoughts." I didn't like admitting that because it made people uptight. But he'd asked.

He widened his eyes. "Can you read mine?"

I smiled. "Sort of." I played it down a bit.

He scowled. "Not sure I like the sound of that."

"He can't read mine that easily." Thompson always loved to announce that. I think he was proud that I couldn't get in his brain without a fight.

"Yes, you're harder for me to read."

"Huh." Jeff pulled his brows together. "Wonder why that would be."

"Some people have more of a wall around their mind." I met Thompson's gloating gaze. "But he's not completely immune to my skills."

Thompson frowned.

"And TV hasn't helped people understand psychics any." I sighed. "Most of the time we're either portrayed as con artists or evil masterminds who want to rule the world."

Jeff grinned and looked at his brother. "So you're dating the Dr. Evil of the psychic world?"

I frowned at his description. "Hey, I'm one of the good guys."

Thompson gave his brother an annoyed glance. "Liam uses his gift to solve violent crimes. He's the furthest thing from evil."

"Sorry. I'm just kidding." He glanced around the booth. "Still, it's kind of creepy to think Liam sees dead people."

I met Jeff's wary glance. "I get your reaction a lot. People treat me like a freak, and most of the cops at the station don't like to talk to me much." I shrugged. "But I'm used to it."

Nodding, Jeff said, "Yeah. People are leery of things they don't understand." He cleared his throat and dropped his gaze to his menu. "Gosh, everything on here looks so good, I can't decide what to get."

I realized he was just trying to change the subject since it made him uncomfortable. He already knew he was getting the Parmesan eggplant. He'd made his decision ten minutes ago before Thompson and I had even arrived. I sipped my tart drink, welcoming the warm tingling sensations that rippled through me from the alcohol. I'd secretly hoped Jeff wouldn't be a skeptic, but he obviously was. And if he was, that meant Thompson's whole family probably was. God, was I going to have to go through a bunch of awkward meetings like this with the rest of the Thompson clan? I took another large slurp of my drink at that thought.

An awkward silence fell. I knew Jeff was both freaked-out by my gift and curious about it. He knew he should probably change the subject because he didn't want to make me feel bad, but he seemed unable to stop thinking about my abilities.

I sighed. "You can ask me questions if you want. I know it's weird that I'm a psychic. But I didn't ask for this. I was born this way."

"I wondered if you were born with it or if it showed up later in life."

"Yes. It runs in my family."

"It can do that?"

"Yep. It moves around from generation to generation. There's no pattern." I picked up my drink and swallowed half of it nervously. I hated so much focus on me. I preferred to be in the background.

"Wow." He squinted at me. "That's so weird."

"It's not to me, but I know it is to everyone else." I grabbed a breadstick from the basket on the table, if only so I had something to do. "We all have different ideas of what is weird or strange. For me, trying to date someone who's close to their family is weird."

Jeff frowned. "Really?"

"Yeah. I wasn't close at all to mine."

"Not at all?"

I shook my head. "But from what Thompson has said, you guys are super, super close. For me that's intimidating. Really nerve-racking even." I sipped my drink some more, probably proving how stressful this all was for me. "I'll take circus freaks like me over trying to understand family dynamics any day."

Jeff didn't respond.

"You're not a circus freak." Thompson's tone was chiding.

I laughed stiffly. "I guess my point is just that I don't know what someone does to fit into a family. It's as alien to me as my psychic abilities are to you guys."

"So... you really aren't close to your family at all?" Jeff seemed puzzled by that concept.

"No. Well, they're dead now. My parents are." My brain felt a little fuzzy from the booze. I hadn't had much lunch, and I couldn't drink much even on a good day.

"Oh, I'm sorry."

"They weren't great people." I laughed tersely, taking another gulp of my drink. I knew I was drinking way too fast, but it tasted good, and I loved the little cozy sensation it gave me of being wrapped in a warm cocoon.

"That's hard for me to picture because our family is so warm and loving." Jeff rubbed his jaw, flicking his gaze to his brother. His concern that I might end up flaking on Thompson came through loud and clear.

"I love your brother," I said abruptly, trying to reassure him.

"Okay." Jeff gave an uneasy laugh.

"I just figured you should know that."

"Thanks."

"No problem. Plus I figured you should know right up front that my family was really different. Because I might have issues from how I was raised."

"Yeah. Sure." Jeff nodded. "When you say your parents 'weren't great people,' what does that mean exactly?"

I didn't love talking or thinking about my dysfunctional family. But since I'd brought it up, I couldn't really avoid answering. Maybe he'd be more patient with me if he knew the details. Maybe.

Shit. I feel pretty drunk.

"Do you mind elaborating?" Jeff nudged.

"Well... my dad was a religious nutcase who thought my psychic abilities came from the devil. Even though this stuff runs in the family, he still liked to pretend it was Beelzebub coming to destroy us all." My laugh was a self-conscious croak.

"Oh, wow."

"Liam—"

I ignored Thompson's warning tone. "Yeah. He was a piece of work." As the booze hit me more, perspiration gathered on my upper lip, and I started babbling. "He wasn't exactly violent, but he definitely liked to use the belt on me if he caught me talking to spirits. God, he hated it when I talked with the spirits. He didn't seem to understand that they reached out to me first." I was definitely feeling tipsy now. As I continued to talk about how awful my dad was, a part of me felt relief. I almost had myself convinced that blurting out every negative thing I could think of about my family all at once would be a good thing. Although, judging from the weirded-out look on Jeff's face, maybe it was a bad strategy.

"Sorry, God, I'm really talking a lot, aren't I?" I winced.

"It's okay," Jeff said.

"Is it?" Thompson laughed.

The vodka was pumping beautifully through my bloodstream now. "My mom was a whore. I'm not exaggerating either. She would screw anybody who'd have her if they gave her money or trinkets."

"Whoa." Jeff laughed awkwardly. "Probably shouldn't call your mom that."

"Well, she was." I finished off my martini.

"Oh, dear," Jeff muttered.

"Slow down there, chief," Thompson said softly.

"These lemon drops are delicious." I sighed.

Thompson grimaced as I signaled for another drink when the waiter walked by. Thompson was well aware I couldn't hold my liquor. In the beginning of our relationship, he'd thought I'd been exaggerating when I'd said it was best if I didn't drink. But since dating me, I'd had enough squabbles with hovering spirits while inebriated that he now believed me.

"You sure you want another drink?" Thompson kicked me gently under the table.

"Oh, yeah." I nodded, my body wonderfully warm from the effects of the alcohol.

Jeff gave another one of his confused laughs.

I bit into my breadstick, and once I'd swallowed, I stupidly continued to talk. "I don't have any siblings, and we never had any pets."

"That's too bad," Jeff said, looking sympathetic.

"Right? I think everybody had a dog but me. But my father thought they were unclean.

'You shall not let those filthy creatures into our blessed home!'" I waved my breadstick, mimicking my dad. "So it was just me and my little ghost friends most of the time growing up." I tried to smile, but I didn't really feel like it, so it came off more like I was baring my teeth.

Thompson snorted and shook his head, but he didn't say anything. I couldn't help but feel that my inability to now shut up was really his fault. Would it have killed him to say a few nice things about me when we'd first sat down? Maybe then I wouldn't have felt the need to fill the awkward silences myself.

"I guess I should ask you about other parts of your childhood, Liam." Jeff smiled at his brother. "But to be honest, I'm kind of afraid to."

My laugh was too loud, and I took my second drink eagerly from the waiter when it arrived. "I really shouldn't drink," I said, sipping my new cocktail.

"He's not lying." Thompson grinned.

Jeff surprised me when he started laughing. "No wonder Denny couldn't compete." He laughed again. "You're very unique, Liam."

"He's really nervous, and he gets weird when he's drunk." Thompson studied me affectionately. "Oh, and one drink gets him drunk."

"Ahhh." Jeff nodded. "That explains a lot."

I met Jeff's gaze. "I am drunk and nervous. I wasn't sure meeting Thompson's family was such a good idea."

"Why?" Jeff narrowed his eyes.

I scowled. "Why? Look at me; I'm sweating and blabbering like an idiot." I turned to the old woman ghost, who was still yelling at her husband about the spaghetti sauce situation. "For the love of God, woman, it's just sauce. Do you seriously think your sauce is the only sauce Waldo should enjoy?"

"Oh, my God." Thompson snorted a laugh. "There he goes."

Jeff scratched his head. "Who is he talking to?"

"Who knows." Thompson continued to grin.

I met Thompson's eyes and laughed sheepishly. "She's really annoying me."

"I can tell." Thompson smirked.

"Those ghosts you mentioned earlier are still in our booth?" Jeff glanced around uneasily. "The old couple?"

"Yes. She really loves her sauce," I muttered.

The waiter came up to take our food order. I was glad for the interruption because it helped take some of the attention off me. By the time the waiter walked away, I felt calmer. Still drunk, but not as uptight.

"Eat your breadstick," Thompson's voice was coaxing as he moved my second martini closer to him. "You need something to soak up the booze in your stomach."

"Okay." I exhaled and nibbled on my breadstick. "I think I've had enough to drink."

Jeff nodded. "Yeah. Let's not do shots." His thoughts were more friendly toward me now than when we'd first met. He definitely thought I was strange, but he liked that Thompson seemed happy and fond of me. He didn't understand the appeal, but he was relieved his brother seemed more settled.

I cleared my throat, feeling like I needed to show Jeff that I was capable of normal conversations too. "I understand that your main concern is that I'm a good fit for your brother." I met Thompson's warm gaze. "I think I am. We seem to make each other happy. Isn't that what it's all about?"

Jeff lifted a shoulder. "In the long run, I guess so."

"I'm not a natural at this meet-the-family thing."

"Seriously? I had no idea." Jeff's lips twitched.

I gave a grudging smile. "At least there are no secrets between us."

"Nope. You got it all out in the first five minutes." Thompson glanced at his watch. "Make that four point five minutes."

"God, I sure hope there are no other secrets." Jeff widened his eyes, looking amused.

My face was hot. "If I ever meet the rest of the family, can we please do it at an AA meeting or something so there's no chance I can get a drink?"

"As strange as you are, my brother has dated worse people."

"True. But I've never brought them to meet you guys." Thompson frowned and glanced at me. "I've never brought anyone to meet my family. Just you."

It pleased me that Thompson wanted me to know that.

Thompson smirked. "And even if Jeff goes home and reports to the rest of the family that you're a nutcase, I still feel lucky to have you in my life, Liam."

I sighed. "Honestly, I feel like the lucky one, Thompson."

Jeff nodded and winked at me. "Good answer. I think I'm gonna like you after all."

****

By the time Thompson and I got back to his place, I was sober and horny. He had no problem with the horny part, since he'd started stripping the second we got to his bedroom. He was naked and on the bed before me, the lube and condom next to him.

"Hurry up, slowpoke," he nagged.

I tossed my shirt onto the end of the bed, staring down at my pale, naked body. My erection sprang proudly between my thighs. "You want a piece of this?" I laughed, gesturing to myself.

"You know I do." His lips twitched. "Maybe even two pieces."

I moved toward him and crawled on the bed, lying beside him. "Did my smooth act at dinner with Jeff get you all hot and bothered?"

He winced. "That was a train wreck."

I covered my face, laughing. "I know. God, he thought I was nuts. I could read his thoughts so plainly." I dropped my hands.

Thompson moved to straddle me, a dark lock of hair on his forehead. "Don't need to be a psychic to know that."

He slipped on a condom and lubed his length. Leaning down, he captured my mouth, and all thoughts of his brother evaporated. I wound my arms around him, moaning into his mouth and aching for more than just kisses. Whenever Thompson entered my body, there was something about it that soothed and excited me. Sex wasn't just about lust with him; it was a connecting of our body and souls, and it was powerful. Earthshaking even.

"Liam," he whispered, smoothing his big hands down my sides and sliding them under my body to squeeze my ass cheeks. He let me read his mind, and his love was raw and warm as it curled like smoke in my brain.

"Me too." I split my legs, rocking my hips as our cocks slid together. "Me too, Thompson."

He kissed me again, pushing his tongue between my lips as I groaned with need. He seemed impatient to get inside me tonight, which was fine by me. Sometimes he took his time about slipping in, but I sensed he needed in me quicker this time. He adjusted his position so that his cock bumped my entrance.

I caressed my hands over his firm pecs and chest, loving the rugged, wide-shouldered masculinity of him. I flicked his beaded nipple with my thumb, and he winced and then laughed. "Tickles?" I asked, teasingly.

"Yeah."

His smile faded as a spark ignited behind his dark eyes. His expression became serious as he pressed his cock to my hole. My heart stuttered with anticipation, and I arched my back and groaned as he entered me. I shuddered at the delicious invasion, dropping my chin so that we held each other's gaze. There was something so intensely personal about him sinking deep into my ass while he watched me. There was nowhere to hide. He had me physically and emotionally captured at that moment.

"I love you." His voice shook as his thick cock stretched me. "Love you so much, Liam." His voice was a growl as he flexed his hips, thrusting deep.

My skin prickled with buzzing need as I clenched my hole on his dick. The friction was so intense, I could barely breathe or form words. But I sensed he needed to hear my feelings, so I swallowed and whispered, "Love you too. With all my heart."

He smiled and started fucking me harder. I lifted my hips, wanting anything he gave me, aching to please him. The muscles of his forearms and neck strained as he pumped into me, his lips parted and sweat beading on his cheeks.

My climax built with each of his thrusts into me, tingling at the base of my cock and then inching up my shaft. The feel of his warm, hard body on mine was all I needed. There were no other thoughts at that moment other than Thompson: the feel of him rubbing against me, the clean scent of his warm skin, and the little grunts of pleasure that came from deep in his throat. I craved Thompson like he was a part of me. The sound of his voice and the caress of his gaze made my soul come alive. I'd felt so crushed and dead after Will died, the thought of going on had seemed too much. But now, nothing could make me let go of Thompson. Absolutely nothing. I felt like even if I died, I'd hover near. Watching over him and keeping him safe.

He lifted his head and looked at me with an urgency that needed no words. My heart squeezed at the intense emotions burning in his eyes. He grunted and came, his cock jerking inside me as he climaxed, pushing me over the edge too. We kissed as our bodies shuddered with pleasure, trembling flesh against flesh so achingly satisfying. My release spilled silently between our quivering torsos, and I moaned and buried my head against his chest. The thump of his heart beneath my cheek was like him: strong and steady.

We held each other for a while, kissing and not saying anything. I felt so content, I almost didn't want to move. But eventually, he pulled out and we got in the shower together. He washed my hair gently, planting soft kisses on my face. He was quiet and his expression serious, but he was so affectionate, I wasn't worried about his feelings for me anymore.

Once we were dry, we got into bed and he wrapped me in his arms. I closed my eyes and exhaled, my muscles tired and loose. All I wanted now was to fall asleep in the arms of my favorite person in the world.

Unfortunately, that's when the vision hit me.

S.C. Wynne

Chapter Seven

The only warning I had that the vision was coming was a slight tingling behind my eyes. But then I was in the middle of a dark alley, with a woman screaming for her life. Her obvious terror slammed through me as I struggled to understand what I was seeing.

The woman clawed at a man who slashed viciously at her throat. She fought so desperately, two of her purple glittered nails broke against his chest. He must have managed to hit her carotid artery, because blood spurted over him. Her eyes widened and she clutched at her throat, but then she tumbled to the ground, and within minutes she was gone.

Panting, the man gasped for air, straightening the hood of his blue sweatshirt and looking around nervously. He was covered in his victim's blood, and I knew he hadn't counted on her putting up such a fight. As he rubbed uselessly at his blood-soaked shirt, behind him a brightly lit billboard poked above the nearest building, announcing outdoor ice-skating at Westfield Topanga. It was a grim juxtaposition: cheery smiling families, and a woman lying on the asphalt, gurgling her last breaths.

The spirit of the woman stood over her corpse. She looked up slowly and stared at me, her expression angry. The man was completely unaware of the spirit as he bent over the body and put something up to her throat. He gagged and wiped his face with the back of his arm, but then he again put something to her gaping neck wound. I couldn't see what it was he held, but it looked really small. He stood and tucked the item in his back pocket, and then he took off on foot away from the murder scene.

An eerie silence fell, and when I blinked, the woman was suddenly next to me. Her black eyes glittered, and her mouth moved stiffly. "Don't you forget about me. Don't you *fuckin'* dare."

"Who are you?" I whispered, trying to kick into gear. Was this a dream? A real murder? I didn't think I was asleep, but my brain felt lethargic.

She leaned closer and snarled, "I matter too."

"Tell me your name."

"Shalondra."

"Liam?" Thompson's worried voice filtered into my consciousness as she began to fade.

"Your full name. *Quickly*," I mumbled.

"I matter too, motherfucker," she hissed and disappeared.

I opened my eyes slowly to find Thompson leaning over me. His eyes were narrowed and his mouth a grim line. "Were you having a bad dream?"

Sitting up, I wiped sweat from my face. "No. I wasn't asleep." I blinked slowly, feeling a little nauseous. "It was a vision."

"Yeah?" He rubbed my back. "What did you see?"

I exhaled roughly, willing my pounding heart to slow down. "I saw a woman being murdered."

"Can you give me some details?" His concerned boyfriend voice had now been replaced by his cop voice.

"The victim was African American, and her throat was cut." I swallowed, remembering the blood pouring from her throat. "Her name was Shalondra."

"Did you get her last name? How about where it happened? Did you recognize any landmarks?" He fired his questions quickly as he rolled off the bed.

I stayed where I was, feeling drained. "I didn't get her full name. She was so angry, she didn't really give me much." I sighed. "The killer seemed green."

"How do you mean?" He pulled on his jeans.

"I could feel his hesitancy and confusion." I closed my eyes and tried to recall anything about the killer that would stand out. "He had a hoodie on, and it covered his face and hair. His build was average, leaning toward slender. Nothing about him was unique."

Thompson had his cell to his ear, and he nodded. When someone came on the line he said, "Have there been any black women found with their throats cut in the last twelve hours?"

"In an alley," I called out.

He repeated my info to the person on the phone. He frowned. "Okay. Thanks." He hung up. "Nothing yet. Maybe the body just hasn't been found."

"Yeah." I frowned. The jangle of his keys made me realize he was getting ready to leave. "Are you going in now?"

"Well, yeah. Aren't you coming with me?"

I wrinkled my brow. "But... I thought we were working Gloria's case."

"We are." He laughed gruffly. "But you saw a murder."

"You think it's connected to Gloria's case?"

"Don't you?"

I got off the bed slowly. "I wasn't thinking they were connected."

He hesitated. "As long as I've worked with you, anytime you witness an actual murder, it's usually somehow a part of the case we're on." He pulled his brows together. "Am I wrong about that?"

I grabbed my shirt and put it on quickly. "I don't know why, but I was thinking this was a separate case. Shalondra was stabbed in the throat while Gloria was strangled."

"But she came to you, Liam." He looked puzzled.

I matter too, motherfucker.

The memory of Shalondra's angry words slammed into me. "Shit. You're right. She came to me."

"Are you feeling all right?"

I shook my head as if clearing cobwebs. "I think so."

"Get some pants on. You can't go to the station like that." His eyes lingered on my boxers.

"Maybe the booze I had messed with my brain." I slipped into my jeans, feeling a little concerned that my first thought hadn't been to connect Shalondra to Gloria's case. "Obviously they're connected."

He moved up to me and put his hands on my shoulders. "You're worrying me, Liam."

"I'm fine. It was just a momentary glitch." I laughed stiffly.

"I sure hope so. I rely on you to help me piece all this psychic shit together."

I rubbed my temples. "Maybe I'm just tired." The images of Shalondra's murder weren't as clear to me as they usually would be. It was as if they were slowly fading from my memory. "I feel like something is wrong."

"What?"

"The details of Shalondra's murder seem to be disappearing from my mind. The visions always fade, but my memory of what I've seen generally stays. But not with Shalondra." I grabbed my phone and turned on the voice recorder as Thompson stared at me, looking puzzled. "Victim is Shalondra. Black. Throat sliced. The guy is thin, nothing special. He bent over her... yeah... he bent over her, and he did something around her throat area." I swallowed and continued. "It was almost like he was taking her blood. Maybe? I don't know. But he did something." I frowned. "Also in the background there was a big billboard." I squinted and tried to recall what I'd seen. "It was advertising ice-skating at Westfield Topanga."

"Really?" Thompson sounded doubtful.

I glanced at him, pausing my recording. "What?"

"It's the middle of February. There's no outside ice-skating in Los Angeles that lasts past January."

"Well, I know what I saw." I frowned. "That sign was definitely advertising ice-skating."

"That doesn't make a lot of sense."

"How often do they change out those signs?"

Thompson scratched his stubbled jaw. "I think the typical term is something like twelve weeks?"

"Do they leave them up even if they're no longer relevant?"

"I have no idea. I guess it depends on how professional the company is."

"It's fading away quickly, but I'm sure I saw ice skating at the Westfield Topanga. Or... shit was it roller-skating?" I scowled and rubbed my head. "No... I'm pretty sure it was ice-skating."

"Is it possible you saw a murder that happened a while ago?"

"That would be unusual. Especially since the spirit reached out to me. Why would she wait?" I scowled.

"No idea. I don't understand dead people. I have enough trouble with the living."

"We'd know a ballpark of when she was murdered if we knew how long those billboards were up. We need to know the company who handled that skating campaign. That would give us a window of time. Maybe we need to call every single billboard company in the city."

He smirked. "Or, we can just call Westfield Topanga and ask when and how long they ran those ice-skating campaigns."

I grimaced. "Well, if you want to take the easy way, sure."

He chuckled, and we headed out the door.

The station was quiet when we arrived, with only a skeleton crew working. There were no reports of an African American female with her throat cut in February. Even though I couldn't understand why a spirit would wait months to approach me, Thompson convinced me to help go through every recorded homicide of black women during December and January. It was dreary work for sure, but I was determined to find the poor woman who'd come to me tonight.

It took hours, but when I finally stumbled across a photo of Shalondra in a morgue head shot, I leaned back in my seat and let out a yelp. "I've got her!"

Thompson rose from his desk and knelt beside me. "Jane Doe #4," he read aloud.

"That's her. I'm sure of it."

He leaned closer. "No ID. No forensic evidence of any kind collected at the scene or on her body. Approximately twenty-five years old."

"God, she looks forty. Why would she be a Jane Doe?" I asked, frowning. "In this day of DNA, how the hell would they not be able to identify her?"

"They may not have had a DNA match… if they tried."

I grimaced. "I think she was a prostitute. I got a really strong sense of that. If she was working the streets, no doubt she's been arrested. You'd think her prints would be in the system even if they didn't get a DNA match."

Thompson glanced up at me, his expression uncomfortable. "Indifference strikes again."

"What does that mean?"

He sighed. "All it takes is someone who thinks she deserved it because she was a hooker, or they're racist, to just drop the ball, and Shalondra becomes Jane Doe #4."

"That's disgusting." I remembered her angry words: *I matter too.*

"It says she was discovered December 25th." He chuffed. "No wonder no one gave a shit."

"Sure. Wouldn't want some poor dead prostitute to interfere with your turkey and stuffing," I growled.

"Well, at least you know her first name. That's a start. I'll check missing persons and see if anyone reported her as having disappeared."

I leaned back in my chair. "I don't understand how Gloria's murder and hers could be connected. They come from two very different worlds."

"If she hadn't come to you, I'd agree."

"She was murdered in December, so why wait till February to come find me?" The murdered spirits usually couldn't wait to get to me. No one waited months.

"Good question. Maybe she just got tired of waiting." He stood. "I'm going to make coffee. Want some?"

"Do you really even have to ask?"

He chuckled and walked away. I got up and grabbed Gloria's case file from his desk and tossed it next to Shalondra's. That's when the second vision of the night hit me. I stumbled sideways, knocking into the chair at the sight of a blonde girl, kneeling and sobbing.

"I don't want to. I don't want to." Her voice shook with terror as the person with her wrapped a belt around her throat. Her attacker wore a black hoodie that obscured his face, but auburn tips of hair poked out around the hood of the sweatshirt.

"You said you believed in fate."

"No," she shrieked, sobbing even louder. "Please."

"This is an honor. Shut up and stop crying." The killer's voice was more of a growl. "Don't you understand the gift you've been given?"

She gagged and gasped for air as the killer squeezed the leather tight. Her eyes bugged, and she scratched at him, her body convulsing as he tightened the belt. She kicked and hissed with a desperation that made me sick to my stomach, and then she fell silent.

The killer stood, breathing hard while staring down at her. "You were chosen," he snapped. Then he pulled a slip of paper and pink feather from his pocket and bent over her. He stuffed both items in her mouth and gave a giggle that sent chills down my spine.

The vision disappeared abruptly, and I leaned against the wall with my eyes wide. My legs seemed to give way, and I slid slowly down until my ass bumped the floor. That tittering laugh had been eerily familiar. "No fucking way," I whispered.

He's in jail. Thompson made sure he's in jail.

Thompson walked into the area, and when he saw me on the floor, he set the coffees down on the desk and then rushed toward me. "What happened?" He sounded breathless as he knelt beside me. "Are you sick?"

I shook my head, sweat trickling down the side of my face. "I might puke, but I'm not sick."

Thompson's face was a canvas of confusion.

"I had another vision." I swallowed, wishing the sound of the young girl's pleading cries would fade away.

"Shit." He grabbed my arm and tugged me to my feet. I swayed and leaned on him, appreciating his steadying arm around me. "Two in one night?"

I nodded, squeezing my eyes shut and willing the sounds of her distraught sobs away. The killer had been so cold and focused, the memory of his voice making me shiver. "I heard his giggle."

"Who?"

I lifted my head and met his dark eyes. "You know who."

Squinting, he said, "Liam. We've been over this already." There was a hint of exasperation nestled in his tone.

I pulled away from him. "I know what I heard." I scowled. "Would you rather I didn't tell you what I feel?" *What I know.*

Pulling his brows together, he shook his head. "No. Of course I want you to be honest with me."

"Then listen when I tell you I know that laugh. I would recognize it anywhere."

His face tensed. "Liam—"

"When he stuffed the note in her mouth… he giggled. It's a very distinctive sound."

"Steven Pine isn't the only guy who has ever had a weird laugh."

I clenched my jaw. "Sorry, but his sick, smug giggle is etched in my memory forever." I flicked my gaze to his. "Also, let's not forget how Gloria said the word 'Pine.'"

He sighed and raked a hand through his shaggy hair. "Jesus, Liam. All of this is scary enough without you telling me Steven Pine can murder people from his jail cell." A muscle worked furiously in his cheek. "That's just too much." His obvious concern filtered over me.

"What if he isn't actually killing them, but he has someone on the outside. Someone who maybe emulates him."

"You shot down my copycat theory."

"Yeah, but I don't just mean someone who worships the guy and copies him. I mean someone who does his actual bidding?" I grimaced and tried to think through my theory. "Maybe this guy is psychically linked to Pine somehow."

"This sounds nuts. You know that, right?" He sighed. "What exactly did you see just now?"

"Well, obviously I saw another girl being strangled. You'll be interested to know it was a different type of belt." I rubbed my temples. "I don't know where they were, but it wasn't the gymnasium. The guy was so cold and calculating, very different from Shalondra's killer." I frowned. "He said she'd been chosen."

"Chosen by who?"

"I don't know. The victim was younger than Shalondra, like Gloria's age."

Thompson's face was scrunched in disgust. "How the hell does Shalondra intersect these murders? If you're right and Shalondra was a hooker, why would the murderer slit her throat and then start strangling these young college girls?"

"I don't know. Practice?"

Thompson winced. "Jesus."

"Shalondra's killer seemed like he was out of his depth. But the guy who killed Gloria and this girl was focused and cold."

"Wait, you think there are two killers?"

I frowned and delved into my intuition deeper. "No. Not really."

"Then I don't understand."

"If it's the same guy, he's different now. That's all I'm saying."

"Okay."

I gave Thompson a wary look. "I... I know in my gut that Pine is involved. I know you don't want to believe me, but I can't shake this horrible churning in my stomach that he's a part of this. Remember Pine said arresting him wasn't the end. Maybe he's found a way to make good on that threat."

His mouth was hard, and I could sense his fear and resistance, but then he slumped and nodded. "Shit. Fine. Let's attack it from your angle. Another girl is dead, and we have nothing. I guess we might as well explore your theory."

I was relieved that stubborn tilt to his mouth was gone. "I don't want it to be Pine." I touched my neck. "I really don't." I shivered at the memory of Steven Pine psychically choking me.

His phone rang and he answered it. He had a short, brusque conversation and hung up. "They found her." He sighed. "In the alley behind the Jack in the Box across from the college."

"Shit. So he is focused on that school."

"Or at least the area around the college."

"Do we know where Shalondra was found?" I asked.

He leaned over and examined the report. "Across town. Nowhere near the college."

"Seriously?"

"Yep."

"Regardless, I know they're connected." I stood, feeling exhausted. Two visions in one night was draining, and I knew when I got to the scene, the new dead girl would probably have something to say to me. I was emotionally depleted, and I really didn't want to have to talk to her. But I didn't have that option, and so I followed Thompson to his car.

The ride to the crime scene was quiet. I didn't know exactly what Thompson was thinking, but I didn't need to read his mind to know he was worried. Two girls dead in two days was bad. Really bad. It meant the killer was in a hurry to make his point. We weren't even close to solving the first girl's death, and now we had a second one. Things weren't going to get easier from here.

The crime scene was buzzing with cops and looky-loos from the nearby fast-food restaurant. We slipped under the tape and made our way toward the body that was covered by a black tarp. My biggest fan, Officer Perrell, was there, and he gave me his usual mocking glance. There was also one forensic investigator placing yellow markers around the corpse.

She glanced up when we approached. "Hey, guys."

"Judy." Thompson stopped next to her. "Strangled?"

"Yep." She sighed. "Young too. Such a shame."

Officer Perrell piped up. "Nobody heard or saw anything." He smirked in my direction. "I mean, not anybody normal. You probably saw something, right, Baker?"

I ignored him and moved closer to the body.

"We can take it from here, Perrell." Thompson's voice was hard. "Why don't you go annoy someone else?"

"I'm supposed to stick near the body. Sorry. I've got my orders."

"It's fine," I muttered to Thompson. "I'll just try and ignore him." I tuned out Officer Perrell's irritating energy as best I could and focused on the tarp. I knelt beside the body and peeled back the plastic. I stiffened at the look of horror on the girl's face. It was definitely the girl from my vision. "Do we know her name yet?"

Judy said, "Valerie Jones. She's eighteen."

"Is she a student at the college across the street?" Thompson asked.

"No idea." Officer Perrell shrugged.

"I was asking Judy," Thompson grumbled.

She shot an irritated glance toward Officer Perrell. "Looks like it. She had a LACC student ID. We also found a piece of paper and a feather in her mouth." Judy grimaced. "Like the last girl."

"Any obvious signs of sexual assault?" I asked.

"Nothing I can see. Obviously the ME will have more details on that. But there are no outward signs."

"Thanks, Judy," Thompson said.

"You got it." She moved away, scanning the area with her flashlight, looking for the smallest details that could help solve the case.

"So the note and feather are an actual tangible connection to Gloria's murder," Thompson said softly.

"Yep." I tugged the tarp back over Valerie's face with a shiver. "Shalondra's report didn't mention anything about a note or feather."

"But was that because they didn't exist, or someone was so sloppy they didn't care to mention it?"

I straightened and turned my back on Officer Perrell and his cynical energy. I centered myself and then whispered, "Valerie. Talk to me." Officer Perrell snorted a laugh, and I clenched my teeth. "If you can't be quiet, you need to move the fuck away."

"Calm down, weirdo." He chuffed.

I glanced over my shoulder, giving him a hard stare. "I don't give a shit if you believe in my abilities or not, but your department does. So if you interfere again, I'm gonna be sure the captain hears about it."

Officer Perrell scowled. "Jesus, you're so touchy."

"I'm trying to solve a murder here." My voice was borderline shrill.

Holding up his hands, Officer Perrell said, "Fine. Have at it."

"What is your deal, Perrell?" Judy shook her head and placed a yellow evidence tent on the ground. "You know we're all on the same team, right?"

Officer Perrell shrugged. "Whatever."

I turned back to the body and closed my eyes, trying to calm my angry pulse. I sucked in a slow breath and said, "Valerie, I'm here if you want to talk to me." This time Perrell kept his mouth shut, although I could feel his derisive thoughts circling me.

It took a few minutes of me muttering how I was here for her, before Valerie showed up. She looked bewildered, similar to how Gloria had been. They both shared a strong sense of betrayal pointed directly at the killer, as if he'd had them thoroughly convinced they could trust him.

"His face was different," she mumbled, glancing around the crime scene. "Not the same. Not the same."

"The person who hurt you, do you know his name? Was he your friend?"

Her face crumpled, and she started crying. "Not him. No."

"I need a name. Let me help you."

She turned her pale, tear-stained face toward me, the veins showing beneath her skin. "Where did he go?"

I frowned. "Who?"

She touched her bruised neck. "Have I been given a gift?"

I didn't know how to respond to her. "Give me a name, Valerie." My voice was urgent. "Please."

"Rusty. Rusty. Our little secret." She put her finger to her lips. "Shhhh. Don't tell. The others will be mad."

"Is that a nickname or his real name?" Murdered spirits' thoughts often jumped around a lot. They were usually traumatized. But Valerie was even harder to pin down than most.

"I'm special?" She started crying again, but then she stopped abruptly and widened her eyes. "Oh, God. He's here, isn't he?"

She vanished.

"*Fuck*." I clenched my hands in frustration as she disappeared, and stood, feeling light-headed.

"Anything?" Thompson asked.

I sighed. "Maybe. I don't know. She said the killer's name was Rusty. At least, I think she was talking about the killer. It was hard to get her to focus." I shivered and scanned the area. "She said he was here. But I don't know if she was being literal or not." None of the faces in the crowd that hovered behind the yellow tape stood out to me. I exhaled, so exhausted I felt sick.

"You look beat." Thompson's voice was low and concerned.

"I'm so tired."

"You should go home and rest." He was worried about me. It showed in the lines around his eyes and the grim tilt of his mouth. "I realize you don't want to sleep, but you look like you're about to topple over."

He knew I needed to stay awake this close to a murder. The murder victim's death replayed over and over in my mind, and I couldn't shut it off. That was another reason I found the whole Shalondra thing unique. I'd seen her murder once, and then everything had begun to fade immediately. That phantom quality of her information had to be because her death was months old.

"I don't want to rest. I want to make some damn headway in this case."

"Yeah, me too. But I don't want you to get sick."

"I'm fine." My voice was gruff. "Do you have the list of kids in that suicide group?" I moved toward the car as I spoke. I had everything I was going to get from the crime scene, and I wanted to sit before I fell down. "Maybe Valerie was in that suicide group too."

Thompson grunted. "That would be nice to have some kind of pattern. Let's see if Percy sent me the list of names like he promised." He scrolled through his phone, frowning.

I slid into the car, and he stood outside, flipping through the menus on his cell. I leaned my head back against the seat and exhaled a long, tired breath. This case was sucking the life out of me. Seeing the victims' deaths and experiencing it with them was grueling and rough on me physically and mentally. I didn't want to complain to Thompson, but I was feeling really edgy and depleted. I didn't quite feel like myself.

Thompson opened the door and got in, his expression emotionless. He didn't start the car; instead he turned to me. "You were right. Valerie was in that group."

"Shit," I said weakly. "So we now know that club is a part of this. Jesus, why? Who the fuck preys on kids already struggling with suicide?"

"Yeah." He cleared his throat. "While I was at it, I also took a closer look at the other names on the list."

"Is that right?"

"Yep. And you might be interested to know there's also a Rusty Myers who belongs to that Always Listening group."

I sat up. "Let's go. Let's talk to him."

Thompson shook his head firmly. "Tomorrow morning. I'm taking you home."

"But—"

"No. You don't have to sleep, but you're resting. Period." He started the car, and I didn't need to read his mind to know there was no arguing with him.

S.C. Wynne

Chapter Eight

The next morning when Rusty Myers opened his front door, it was obvious he'd been asleep. His eyes were red and puffy, and his brown hair stood straight up. He yawned and took in Thompson's badge without any indication that it made him nervous.

"Did someone vandalize the laundry room again?" He stood on his tiptoes trying to see past us. "They need to put in an alarm or something."

"We're not here about the laundry room." Thompson tucked his badge away.

"Oh." Rusty frowned.

When I probed his mind, there was nothing there even close to resembling guilt. He was simply confused by why we were here. "Do you know a Valerie Jones?" I asked, still tuned in to his energy.

He nodded. "Yes." His mind jumped immediately to Gloria's murder, and the first hint of worry fluttered toward me. "Why?"

Thompson glanced around the small apartment stoop. "Do you mind if we come inside and talk to you?"

"Oh, sure." Rusty moved into the apartment, heading toward the kitchen. "Is it okay if I make coffee while we talk? I have to be at work in a few hours, and my brain is still asleep."

"Go for it," Thompson responded.

Rusty grabbed a bag of coffee from a cupboard over the microwave. He then poured the preground coffee into a paper filter and inserted it into the coffee maker on the counter. "I don't know Valerie well." His anxiety was higher now, and I could feel it growing as he faced us.

"You must have also known Gloria Handy?" I asked. "From your Always Listening group?"

He nodded. "Yeah, I knew her." He swallowed hard. "Did... did something else bad happen?"

Thompson didn't beat around the bush. "Valerie was found murdered last night."

Rusty's eyes widened, and he leaned back against the counter. "Oh, my God." He was sincerely horrified and shocked at the news of Valerie's death. "But how? Why?" He sounded breathless as he stared at us for answers.

"Did you know her well?" Thompson asked, not addressing his questions.

Pulling his brows tight, he said, "Well, we all know a lot of personal stuff about each other." He glanced up. "It's the nature of that kind of group. But I didn't hang out with her, or Gloria, outside of that setting."

"So you've never grabbed coffee with either of them?" I asked softly.

He shook his head. "No. We were really different people. I read a lot and don't like to go out. They were both more... social." His face was a little pink. "I can't believe someone would hurt either of them. They were both really nice."

Thompson glanced at me, and I shook my head. Whether his name was Rusty or not, there was no way this guy was a vicious murderer. He didn't have a hint of meanness in his energy. He was a loner, and he worked at the bookstore on campus. He'd struggled with suicidal thoughts after breaking up with his girlfriend of two years, and he had a good relationship with his mom. Not exactly the bio of a serial killer.

"Is there anyone in the group who makes you feel uneasy?" Thompson asked. "Maybe they have anger issues or something like that?"

"Not really. Everybody is pretty chill. I mean, the weirdest person in the group is no doubt Percy."

"You mean the kid who started the group?" Thompson asked.

"Yeah. But I don't mean he has any anger issues or anything. Mostly he's just anal about a lot of stuff."

"Anal how?"

He lifted one shoulder. "Well, he's controlling. He won't let anyone date in the group. I kind of get his point—if people date and then break up, it could fuck up the group's serenity." He scrunched his face as if deep in thought. "Let's see, how else is he anal? Oh, he only allows snacks outside, because he hates crumbs. He makes us take our shoes off when we come in to the meeting. I can't see him killing anyone. It would be too messy. Percy is borderline prissy."

"Do you get along with Percy?" I asked.

"Oh, yeah. He's cool, overall. Like I said, he worries about the little stuff too much, but he's part of the reason those of us in the group are all still here on earth, ya know? He brought us all together."

I nodded. "So you feel like you owe him your loyalty?"

He frowned. "I don't know if that's the right word. I owe him my gratitude, and if he needed my help, I'd be happy to give it."

"So getting back to Gloria and Valerie—" Thompson interjected.

Rusty's face fell. "Oh, God, yeah."

"You can't think of anyone in the group who would want to hurt them?"

"No. We all got along great." He turned to the coffee maker and cussed. "Damn, I forgot to add the water." He grabbed the empty carafe and filled it at the sink. Then he poured the liquid into the reservoir and pressed the Power button.

"Were you aware Gloria was secretly dating someone in the group?"

He looked surprised. "No way would Percy let that happen."

"I think that's why it was secret," I said.

"But... Percy would know. He knows everything that goes on."

"Apparently not. When we talked to Percy, he didn't seem to have any idea Gloria was dating someone in the club." Thompson studied Rusty. "Maybe Valerie was seeing the same person."

He shook his head slowly. "No. You guys must have it wrong. No one in our group would hurt a hair on either of those girls' heads."

"We already know Gloria was seeing someone from the group, and we know that the person who killed her was someone she trusted and was romantically involved with. We're just trying to figure out who it could be."

Rusty looked like he felt sick. "I can't believe that. We all know and care about each other."

I sighed. "I saw it with my own eyes, Rusty."

He scowled. "What?"

"Liam is a psychic." Thompson shifted uneasily. "He saw both girls die."

The blood drained from Rusty's face, and he stared at us. "Jesus. You saw that?"

"Yes."

"That's horrible."

I nodded. "Yeah."

"Wait a minute." He pulled his brows tight. "Are you speaking to everyone in the group?"

"Yes. We will," Thompson said.

"But you came to see me first?"

I shook my head. "No. Not first."

"But almost first, right?" He sounded breathless. "Why? Why did you come here before talking to some of the others? Do you think I'm the killer?" His voice squeaked.

"We're going to talk to everyone, Rusty." Thompson sounded irritable.

Rusty's thoughts were going a million miles a minute. He was freaked-out and couldn't understand why we were on his doorstep. But even as jumbled as his thoughts were, none of them had anything to do with feeling guilty.

I felt bad for him, so I wanted to explain why we were there before talking to the others. "Valerie said the name 'Rusty.'" His expression tensed. "That's why we're here sooner than we might have been."

He bugged his eyes. "I didn't kill her!" He looked around, panicked. "I swear on my life, I'd never do anything like that to anyone."

I believed him. "We had to follow up. I needed to meet you and see what I could sense about you."

He squinted. "Really?"

"When we saw the name Rusty on the list of members in the group, well, we had to follow the lead." I sighed.

Thompson still watched Rusty suspiciously. "Rusty isn't a very common name."

Rusty glanced at him. "I know."

"So I have to ask, did you see Gloria the night she was murdered?" Thompson asked.

"The last time I saw Gloria was Monday night at our group. I told you, we didn't socialize outside of that club."

"Do you happen to know where you were Wednesday night between 9:00 p.m. and 6:00 a.m.?" Thompson asked.

Rusty licked his lips nervously. "Wednesday? I have classes from nine till ten thirty." He hesitated. "And I met up with my ex after that." His face flushed, and he dropped his gaze as if embarrassed.

"What time did you and your ex say good night?" I asked.

He gave a stiff laugh. "She left about five in the morning." He raked a hand through his messy hair. "We kind of have trouble letting go."

My heart tugged at how vulnerable he sounded. "Okay." It would be a rough feat to have rushed over to murder Gloria right after his girlfriend left. Not to mention he was blond. I realized the killer could wear a wig, but this guy just didn't seem like a murderer to me. "Would you mind giving us her name so we can verify your alibi?"

"Sure." He shrugged. "We're both single still. I don't think she'd care if anyone knew where she was."

"What about last night?" Thompson asked gruffly. "Can you tell us your movements?"

He nodded. "I didn't have class, but I belong to a book club. We meet at seven, and some of us went out for pie and coffee after. I got home around one thirty this morning?"

"That's kind of late for pie and coffee, isn't it?" Thompson frowned.

"Well, we were dissecting this James Patterson mystery we read." His eyes shined with excitement. "He actually has you inside the head of one of the characters when he kills the guy. I mean that's nuts."

My lips twitched at his unbridled enthusiasm. Thompson didn't look nearly as amused. I sensed his impatience at how everyone we'd interviewed so far seemed like they couldn't possibly be involved in these two murders.

"Can I have your girlfriend's number?" Thompson asked.

"Oh, yeah." Rusty moved to a small desk and grabbed a Post-it note. He wrote down the number and handed it to Thompson. "I didn't hurt those girls. I swear. But if there's anything I can do to help you catch the monster who did, just ask. I mean absolutely anything."

Thompson sighed. "Thanks."

We left Rusty's apartment, and once in the car, Thompson groaned. "How can two girls be dead, but everyone we talk to seems innocent?"

"There are still plenty of people to talk to. We've barely scratched the surface."

"Yeah, that's the fucking problem, Liam. We've barely scratched the surface, and two girls are already dead. At this rate, by the time we're halfway through talking to people, it could be a dozen."

"We need to figure out how these two girls intersect with Shalondra's murder. I know there's a connection. But I don't know what it is yet."

"I checked over all the missing person's reports for the last six months. No one named Shalondra was reported missing."

"Maybe Shalondra was just her hooker name."

"Could be." He started the car. "I've asked the ME to see if we can get a hit on her prints. If we at least had a family member to talk to, it might help."

"I'll take any help we can get right now."

"Me too. Tim Hernandez should be at the station to talk to us when we get back. Maybe he'll be helpful."

"Oh, great." I tried to hide it from Thompson, but the idea of talking with Tim and trying to tap into his mind was exhausting. I wasn't sure why I was still so tired. I'd slept for six hours last night, which was pretty good for me. But my spirit felt heavy and bogged down, as if I was carrying a sack of cement on my shoulders.

Maybe Thompson sensed my struggle, because he glanced over at me. "Let's stop at Jamba Juice and get you a smoothie."

I laughed. "What?"

"You look like you're dragging."

I sighed. "Maybe I'm low on iron or something."

"Even more reason to get you a healthy snack." He turned in to a shopping center as he spoke. He parked and glanced over. "You stay here and rest, I'll grab the drinks."

I watched him walk into the small shop, his stride confident. My chest squeezed with affection. It was hard to believe he was the same man I'd thought was so gruff and unemotional. He was actually extremely nurturing and attentive, something he hid well beneath his brusque exterior. I couldn't even imagine what my life would have been like after losing William, if not for Thompson. He'd saved me. He'd shown me there was still plenty in life to make it worth living.

My mind drifted to the Always Listening group. Why would anyone prey on suicidal kids? What would drive that sort of cruel impulse? If it was a club member, they'd have to be horribly cold and calculating. How could they face the other members knowing they had brutally slaughtered two of their own? So far, no one we'd interviewed had come across to me as capable of killing Gloria or Valerie.

Or Shalondra. Don't forget about me, motherfucker.

That thought banged through my head as if she'd actually growled those words into my ear. I sat up and glanced around, feeling uneasy. It almost felt as if Shalondra's energy was with me still. I'd never had a spirit linger. They always moved on. But I had trouble shaking the sensation that Shalondra was near.

I felt like an idiot, but I said softly, "Shalondra?" When only silence met me, I gave a gruff laugh. But after a few minutes the hairs on the back of my neck stiffened, and a chill filled the car. I frowned and flicked my gaze to the back seat warily. My eyes widened with shock when the fuzzy image of Shalondra materialized, looking pissed. "What the hell?" I yelped.

Her dark eyes slid to me, and for a second, she seemed almost as shocked to see me as I was her. "You again?" The deep, bloody slash in her throat flapped as she spoke.

It took me a few tries to get my question out. "Wh… why are you here?" *How are you here?* I'd never had a murdered spirit on a case come to me more than once. I hadn't even realized they could return.

"Why the hell don't nobody care about me?" A vein in her forehead stood out, and her eyes glittered with anger. "I was murdered. Why don't nobody care about that?"

As freaked-out as I was, I took a deep breath and tried to focus. This was an amazing opportunity to get more information. Just because she apparently didn't follow the usual rules and just showed up whenever she wanted, that didn't mean I shouldn't still communicate with her. "Why did you wait so long to come to me?"

"Baby, I don't even know who the fuck you are."

I frowned. "Then why are you here?"

"Hell if I know. I didn't come here on purpose." Her tone was raspy.

"Really?" I scratched my head. "Well, you must need to talk to me. You must have information for me. That's how it usually works."

"How what usually works? All I know is some motherfucking white dude slit my throat, and ain't nobody give a shit about it for months."

I winced at her angry energy. "I think your death is connected to another case I'm working on." I spoke quietly, hoping she'd take my lead and calm down a little. "Did you know your killer? Can you give me any details?"

"Nobody cared. How fair is that?" She still sounded mad, and she didn't seem to be listening. "What am I, a piece of garbage you just throw away? I'm a person, God damn it." She frowned. "Well, I was a person." She held out her hands. "I don't know what the fuck I am no more."

"Shalondra, do you want my help?" I leaned toward her, hoping to get her attention focused back on me. Most spirits I dealt with on these cases were more bewildered than furious. Maybe her anger was what allowed her to hang around longer than the others, but it was also making her difficult to talk to. "I can help you if you'll let me. Did you see your killer clearly?"

She blinked several times and then seemed to notice me again. "The killer? Yes. I saw him."

"Tell me about him."

"What else do you need to know? The motherfucker sliced me." Her lips quivered with anger.

I grimaced. "Had you ever seen him around before? Do you have a name?"

She scowled. "Do I have a name? What the fuck? Do you think I keep a Rolodex or something?"

I gritted my teeth and held on to my patience. "What did he look like? Can you at least tell me that?"

"I can tell you he didn't look dangerous. Boy was I wrong." She pulled her brows together. "But he was nervous. He practically pissed his pants when he cut me."

"Can you describe him physically?" As hard as she was to talk to, I felt almost giddy. I'd never been able to question a murder victim on one of our cases for over a few moments. This was an amazing opportunity to try and get actual details. But I was so excited, I almost couldn't think what to ask her.

"He was some skinny ginger kid. Looked young as shit. Said he wanted a BJ, but when we got in the alley, he didn't want me to touch him." She frowned. "He was pale and sweaty. But then a lot of guys are the first time they come to me."

I perked up at her mention of his hair color. "He had red hair?"

"Yes." She huffed. "I didn't know the little fucker was gonna kill me, or maybe I'd have paid more attention to him." Her anger boiled over again, and I winced at the harsh energy.

"Can you tell me anything else? Did he have any scars or moles, maybe a tattoo?"

She cackled. "A tattoo? He wasn't the tattoo type."

I felt anxious when I noticed she seemed to be fading. "Is there anything else you can tell me that stood out to you?"

She scowled. "Before he started slicing at me, he said he was sorry. If you're so sorry, then don't stab me, you motherfucker."

He'd said he was sorry? That didn't sound like Pine.

"Do you know why he did it?"

She curled her lips. "I assume it was some satanic ritual."

"Why would you say that?"

"Because he took my blood." She touched her slit throat and pulled her brows tight. "He put some blood in a little vial. Who would do that other than a freakin' devil worshiper?"

That must have been what he was doing when he'd bent over her. "I'm glad you've told me all of this, Shalondra. It could help catch him."

She grunted. "I wasn't going to wait forever." She looked around with a confused expression. "I matter too."

"I agree." I saw Thompson approaching the car, and I glanced at Shalondra. She looked extremely transparent now. "Can you just come to me anytime you want?"

She frowned. "I already told you I didn't come here on purpose. I just show up places."

"Where are you when you aren't here?"

"Nowhere." Her dark gaze was blank. "I ain't nowhere at all."

I was fascinated with her ability to show up in different places. But it was obvious she didn't even know how she did it. "Do you talk to other psychics?"

"What?" She smirked. "Baby, I don't believe in psychics."

When Thompson opened the door, Shalondra disappeared.

I bit back my frustration and took the drinks from him so he could get in the car without spilling them.

"It was packed in there. Jesus, noisy too. That music gave me a headache." He glanced at me and frowned. "You okay?"

"I uh…" I gave a gruff laugh. "I just had a visit from Shalondra."

He widened his eyes. "What? Here?"

"She popped up in the back seat."

He scowled. "Very funny." He took his drink from me with a shake of his head.

"I'm not kidding."

"Seriously?" He unwrapped his straw and stuck it through the lid. It made a loud squeaking noise as he stared at me. "You're telling me you had a ghostly visitor while I was inside Jamba Juice?"

I laughed. "It surprised me too. She isn't following the usual rules."

"Can she do that?"

"She is doing it. I have no idea how."

He straightened, looking excited. "Well, that's great, right? If she can come and go as she pleases, hopefully she can help us."

"I hope so. She's really angry though. It interferes a bit."

"Huh. Well, I'd be pissed too if someone murdered me." He gestured toward my untouched smoothie. "Drink."

"She had some useful information." I peeled the paper wrapper and stuck the straw in the drink. Then I glanced up and met his alert gaze. "Angry or not, she should be able to help us."

"You're sure you didn't just fall asleep and her supposed visit was a dream?"

I frowned. "Why are you doubting me?"

"I'm not. But you were ready to doze off when I left you."

I sucked on my smoothie, kind of annoyed with him but still enjoying the sweet yet tart flavors. Once I'd swallowed I said, "I was wide-awake."

"Okay. Well, what did she say that was useful?" His cheeks hollowed as he sucked on his straw.

"Her killer had red hair."

His eyes brightened. "Yeah?"

"And she said the killer put some of her blood in a little vial."

"Eww." He cringed.

I laughed at his reaction. "Yeah. Creepy. Why do you suppose the killer would take some of her blood?"

"No idea."

I sucked on my straw, thinking about all the possibilities. "It wasn't much blood. Can you do a satanic ritual with just a drop of blood?"

He grinned. "You think I'm an expert on satanic rituals? Most of my info comes from movies."

"Most of it?"

He winced. "All of it."

I smiled.

He glanced at his watch and then set his drink in the cup holder and started the car. "We need to get to the station so we can talk to Tim Hernandez."

"Oh, yeah. I'd forgotten about him."

He backed out of the parking space and then pulled onto the street. "Drink your smoothie. I had them put extra blueberries in yours to protect your brain cells from free-radical damage. Blueberries are full of antioxidants."

"Wow. You take your smoothies seriously."

"Yes I do." He pushed his tongue in his cheek. "Your thirtieth birthday is coming up soon, isn't it? Blueberries are also important for senior health."

"Ha. Ha. You're a riot."

He smirked. "Well, you have looked a little ragged around the edges the last few days."

I grimaced. "Don't do that worrying thing, Thompson. I can feel your concern, and it gives me anxiety."

"Fine. I'll stop worrying if you drink your smoothie like a good boy."

I rolled my eyes.

He glanced over, and when he spoke, he used his bossy cop voice. "I'm serious. Drink your damn smoothie, Liam."

I suppressed a laugh. "Whatever you say, Mom."

S.C. Wynne

Chapter Nine

Tim Hernandez was hiding something. He was difficult to read, and he didn't make eye contact easily. Unfortunately, he didn't just announce that he was our guy either, so we had to do our jobs and try to figure out his guilt or innocence the old-fashioned way.

"Thanks for coming in, Tim." Thompson fiddled with a stack of papers in front of him. "We appreciate your time."

"Sure. Couldn't very well say no, could I?"

I frowned at Tim's resentful tone. His obvious displeasure at speaking with us seemed odd, considering his friend had been murdered. "I would think you'd want to talk to us. You were good friends with Gloria, right?"

"Yes."

"How about Valerie?"

"We were friends, but I was closer to Gloria." He dropped his gaze to the tabletop, looking glum.

"Can you think of any reason why anyone would want to hurt Gloria?" Thompson asked.

"No. But I know her boyfriend, Kyle, was an asshole and he was cheating on her," he growled. His accusatory tone made it clear he suspected Kyle had been involved in Gloria's death.

"Did Gloria know about Kyle's cheating?" Thompson asked.

"I think she suspected. But for whatever reason, she hadn't officially ended it with him yet."

I winced as his intense bitterness wafted over me. "You wanted her to dump him?"

"Of course. He was a douche."

"So it made you mad that she wouldn't break up with him?" Thompson's voice was pointed.

Tim gave my partner a wary glance. "It didn't make me happy."

"Why do you think she put up with Kyle's antics?" I asked.

He sighed. "They'd been together since high school. She didn't know how to say goodbye. But I know she'd started pulling away some. She'd met someone new, and I think that gave her the strength to at least consider ending it with Kyle."

"So you didn't care that some other guy just waltzed in when she was about to maybe end things with Kyle?" I studied him closely. His anger and confusion jumbled around inside him so intensely, I was able to pick up on it. "Especially after you'd waited patiently in the wings for such a long time?"

He hardened his jaw. "I just wanted her to be happy. Kyle didn't make her happy."

"But this new guy did?" Thompson asked.

"She seemed better."

Thompson narrowed his eyes. "And that didn't bug you at all?"

"What are you two implying?" he snapped.

"Simply that it must have hurt a hell of a lot that you were there for her all that time, but she didn't see you romantically. Instead she switched over to some new guy." Thompson's tone was challenging.

"And you think I killed her in a jealous rage?" He scowled. "I wouldn't do that. I wouldn't ever do anything to hurt Gloria. I wanted her happy, and if this new guy did that for her, then that was fine by me."

He seemed sincere. Thompson glanced over at me, and I shrugged. "I think he's telling the truth."

Tim scowled. "Of course I am."

"We need a name." Thompson's voice was hard. "I don't suppose you have one, do you?"

"No."

"He's lying." I could feel his dishonesty from across the table.

Tim glanced up angrily. "Says who?"

Thompson responded first. "Tim, you can get in a lot of trouble withholding information from the police."

He chewed the inside of his cheek as he held Thompson's steady gaze.

"We're just trying to find whoever it was who killed Gloria," I said softly.

"We need a name." Thompson leaned toward him.

He sighed and rested his elbows on the table. "Look... she wouldn't tell me who it was, okay?"

I wiggled deeper into his thoughts. "But you have an idea?"

He pressed his lips tight, looking anxious.

"Tim, you need to talk to us. You have an idea of who she was seeing, right?"

Scowling, he said. "Maybe."

Thompson straightened, his gaze alert. "If you know who she was seeing, you need to tell us. There's a very strong possibility he's the one who killed her."

"What?" He looked taken aback. "No. No. That can't be right."

"She trusted whoever killed her. Same with Valerie. We believe they were both seeing someone in your suicide group," I said.

He didn't look surprised by my revelation.

"Why do I get the feeling you already knew that?" Thompson's gaze never left Tim.

Tim's unwillingness to open up surprised me a little. It was obvious he'd been in love with Gloria. Why was he being so obstinate? "We think the odds are good they were seeing the same guy."

"I wouldn't know."

"Right," chuffed Thompson.

His stubbornness finally got to me because if he had a name, we'd needed that information yesterday. "We don't have time for you to play coy, Tim. How can you sit there in silence when you might know the name of your friend's murderer?"

"I'm not playing coy."

"Then tell us a name," Thompson said tersely.

"I don't want to get anyone in trouble."

"Withholding that person's identity could get another person killed. Is that what you want, Tim?" Thompson voice was a low rumble. "Maybe if you'd come forward immediately after Gloria was killed, Valerie would still be alive."

Tim wilted a little. "God, don't say that."

Thompson hesitated, softening his voice slightly. "Every second we waste means other people might die. We need to bring this person in before he hurts anyone else."

Swallowing, Tim said, "The thing is, Gloria was flirting with a lot of guys. She was even doing it with... with me." His heartbreak wafted off him like fog, and I winced at how devastated he was.

"She wasn't just flirting with whoever killed her," Thompson said.

Tim grimaced. "Still... it's not like I have proof. I just had a feeling that Gloria was getting really close with this person."

"Maybe you're just pretending you know the name of her new boyfriend to throw us off the scent." Thompson narrowed his eyes.

"That's not true." Tim looked pale.

"Did you feel played by Gloria?" Thompson lifted one brow. "Maybe you wanted to get even with her for leading you on?"

"You need to stop saying shit like that." Tim scowled. "There's no way I'd hurt Gloria. Besides, I wasn't even in town Wednesday night. I was on a camping retreat in Big Bear with my church."

"We'll need the name of your pastor so we can double-check that," Thompson said brusquely.

Tim just nodded.

"You need to worry about yourself right now, not this person you're protecting." I spoke softly, taking a less aggressive approach than Thompson, hoping to coax the information out of him. "If there really is another guy, you need to tell us who he is. Who was Gloria seeing on the side?"

He sighed. "But I told you, I don't have any proof."

"Just tell us what you know." Thompson sounded impatient.

Tim exhaled. "There was just something about the way they were together... it just set off my alarms."

"Give us a *name*," Thompson said brusquely.

Tim exhaled. "Percy Johnson."

I wrinkled my brow, surprised to hear his guess. "Percy? The leader of the group?"

"Yes."

Thompson also wore a dubious expression. "What did you see that made you suspect Gloria was seeing Percy?"

"I left my coat in the meeting room one night, and when I went back to get it, I found Gloria and Percy standing super close and whispering. There was just something about the way he had his hand on her arm, and how pink her cheeks were." He shook his head. "I don't know... it was just intimate. You know?"

He sounded so sincerely disgusted, I had trouble not believing him.

"Do you think Percy could be violent?" Thompson asked.

"I don't know. Not really. He's never even raised his voice around me."

I met Thompson's wary gaze. "Percy's mom confirmed his alibi for Wednesday and last night."

Thompson chuffed. "Yeah. No mother ever lied for their kid before."

Tim frowned. "I just don't think Percy would hurt Gloria or Valerie. Sure, maybe he broke his own rules and he was seeing them, but no way would he kill them." Tim sounded convinced, and his thoughts supported his complete faith in Percy's innocence.

"It would have been pretty embarrassing for Percy if word got out he was seeing two of the members." Thompson studied Tim as he spoke.

I nodded. "Especially after he forbade anyone else in the group from dating."

"Yeah. Maybe he wanted to shut Gloria and Valerie up." Thompson's gaze was bright.

"To the point that he'd kill them?" Tim shook his head. "I can't see him doing that."

Thompson leaned toward Percy. "Maybe Gloria and Valerie found out about each other and they confronted Percy. Maybe they had a big fight and it turned violent."

Tim scowled. "But they died on different nights. If he was afraid of them speaking out, wouldn't he have killed them both at the same time?" Tim's voice wobbled. "Plus, he started a suicide group to *stop* people killing themselves. Someone who'd do that isn't likely to then start murdering the members. Right?"

You have a point.

"Probably not," Thompson grudgingly agreed.

I cleared my throat. "I find it hard to picture Percy seducing Gloria and Valerie. He doesn't exactly strike me as a lady's man. Why would both Gloria and Valerie be interested in him romantically?" Both girls had seemed to be out of Percy's league.

Tim shrugged. "When you have power, girls like it."

"Power?" Thompson arched a brow.

"You know, he's in charge of the group." Tim sighed. "He's kind of our hero because that club saved us. We all struggled so much before we found each other. Percy is an authority figure, and chicks dig that."

Percy and authority figure didn't really belong in the same sentence if you asked me. "Did you ever see him acting touchy-feely with Valerie?"

"No. Just Gloria."

Thompson studied him. "Was it just that one time you saw Percy and Gloria together that made you suspicious about their relationship?"

"Well, it made me start paying attention. And once I did that, I could see that they were way closer than I'd ever suspected."

"I see." Thompson nodded. "Okay. Well, we appreciate you coming in and talking to us, Tim. I know this wasn't easy for you. But every little bit helps us close in on the killer. I promise you that."

"I hope so." Tim's energy seemed defeated now. "I still can't believe Gloria is dead. She was so full of life."

His depressed energy concerned me a little. I hoped he wouldn't try and hurt himself because of his friend's death. "We'll get whoever did this, Tim. Don't get discouraged."

He glanced up. "I just miss her, you know?"

I nodded. "Yeah. I get it." He had no idea how much I got it.

He clenched his jaw and then flicked his gaze to Thompson. "Can I go now?"

Thompson stood. "Sure. If you think of anything else that might be helpful, don't hesitate to reach out."

"Okay." Tim left the room, his shoulders bowed.

Thompson slumped back onto his chair with a loud grunt. "God, could Percy actually be our guy?"

"It's hard to believe. He seems so bland and... un-killer-like."

Thompson nodded. "Agreed."

"I seriously didn't get anything off him that would lead me to believe he's capable of murder."

Thompson nodded. "Not to mention Nordstrom's said they'd sold over a hundred of those belts during that weekend sale."

"Yeah, and Valerie's killer used a different style belt."

He rubbed his face with both hands. "But if Tim is right about who Gloria was seeing, that means Percy lied about dating Gloria and probably Valerie."

"Which doesn't necessarily make him a murderer. If he was afraid of being blamed for their deaths, he might lie. People lie a lot just to get out of trouble."

"Yes. If my twelve years on the force have taught me anything, it's that people lie."

"Also sleeping around and murdering people are pretty different. It takes a certain kind of person to kill someone. Percy's weird, but he seemed harmless."

"But you've been fooled before." Thompson's voice was pointed.

I winced. "Yes I have." Pine had fooled me many times by blocking my abilities.

He stood. "How about we comb over everything forensics has for us from both murders? There's got to be something there that will show us where to look next."

I glanced around the room warily. "Let's not forget Shalondra. She wouldn't like that."

"No. We don't want to forget her. I'll keep searching for something that connects the cases."

We went back to Thompson's desk. While he read over the physical evidence gathered so far, I tried once more to get something psychically from the feathers and notes that the killer had stuffed in the victim's mouths. But no matter how hard I concentrated, there just wasn't anything there for me to pick up on.

I fingered the evidence bag that held one of the notes. "These questions are so bizarre."

"Yeah." Thompson had on a pair of reading glasses that he only wore when his eyes were really tired. They gave him a sexy, nerdy vibe. "Why ask them if they believe in fate?"

"So he can throw it back in his victim's face? Remember the killer basically reminded Valerie that she'd said she believed in fate. I guess he was trying to say her death was preplanned by the universe or something."

"Maybe Gloria said she believed in fate too."

"He might choose his victims based on their answers to the questions."

Thompson pulled off his reading glasses. "You mean, if they said they don't believe in fate, he might spare them?"

Grimacing, I said, "Maybe. Who knows? He's obviously nuts. Asking them if they trust him right before he strangles them... that's pretty twisted."

"And you still believe that Pine is involved somehow?" His voice was soft.

I gave him a guarded look. "You know I do." It wasn't even a choice. When we'd arrested Steven Pine months ago, I'd prayed I'd never have to see that sicko again. But I couldn't escape the nagging feeling that he was a part of these girls' deaths.

He pinched the skin between his eyes and grunted. "I said I was willing to look at this case from your angle, and I meant it."

"I appreciate that."

"But I won't lie; I hope you're wrong."

"Yeah, me too."

He pursed his lips. "So if Percy is our killer, how would he be connected to Pine?"

"No idea." I tossed the little evidence bag down. "Has Pine had any visitors other than his lawyers?"

"You mean like Percy?"

"Him, or anyone."

"Probably. The Night Stalker got married in jail. There are lots of weird people out there who are attracted to, and fascinated by, psychos."

I shivered. "I don't get it."

"Me neither." His lips twitched. "I'll take a sexy, self-conscious psychic who can't hold his liquor any day."

I laughed. "Thanks."

He smiled, and then his expression became more serious. "If we're really examining that angle, it's easy enough to check the visitors log for who's been to visit Pine."

"Yeah, it would be awesome if Percy Johnson's name was on that list."

"What are the odds?"

"Probably not good." I rubbed my thumb over one of the bagged feathers, frustrated that I couldn't get any information from it.

Thompson's phone rang and he answered tiredly, but then he sat up straight. "When? Where is he?" He listened to the person on the other end of the line. "We'll be right there."

I leaned toward him. "What is it?"

He slid his phone into his pocket and stood. "Percy Johnson was just attacked on campus."

"Seriously?"

"Yeah. Let's go."

"Jesus." I followed him to the elevator. "Is he okay?"

The elevator doors opened and we got in. "I didn't get a lot of details, but I know he's alive." When the elevator reached the ground floor, we hurried out to the parking lot.

"I'm amazed at how active this perp is. He doesn't even let the dust settle and he's on to the next victim."

"Fortunately, Percy was able to fight off his attacker. I'm hoping we can get some details from him." Thompson unlocked the car, and we got in. He pulled onto the main road and drove swiftly, his jaw clenched.

"Well, I guess this probably means Percy isn't the killer."

Thompson didn't respond.

"Why would the killer attack Percy?" I shifted in my seat to face him.

"Good question."

"Maybe he thinks Percy knows something." I grimaced. "You don't suppose Percy was also dating the killer, do you? Maybe he's bisexual."

Thompson chuffed. "If so, that guy gets around."

"There's also the possibility that Percy could have faked an attack."

"You mean Percy is the killer, and he pretended to get attacked to throw us off his scent?"

"Why not?"

"It's possible. Although, it seems like something that would happen in a TV show more than real life." He braked hard and made a sharp turn into the medical complex.

I braced myself as he wound around the parking structure quickly, searching for a parking space. "Come on. Are you telling me no one in real life has ever faked an attack on themselves, just to get the cops to start looking elsewhere?"

"No. It's happened plenty." He slid the car into an empty spot and shut off he engine. Without waiting a beat, he got out gracefully, and I followed.

I was breathless as I tagged along behind him. "So it's possible that's what Percy did?"

He glanced at me. "Let's hold off jumping to conclusions."

"I'm just throwing out theories."

"I know. I'm simply saying let's talk to the guy and see just how banged up he is. If he's on death's door, he probably didn't do this to himself."

"True," I said agreeably. It just seemed a little too coincidental to me that Percy was suddenly attacked the minute we were about to look closer at him. But I wasn't going to say that to Thompson since he already seemed to think I was rushing to judgment.

The nurses' station was able to tell us what room Percy was in. When we entered the room, there was a nurse fiddling with an IV bag next to the bed. Percy had his eyes closed, and his skin was so pale his red hair stood out glaringly. The entire left side of his face was swollen and purple, and there were deep red gouges around his neck.

Looking up, the nurse frowned. "He's resting." Thompson showed her his badge, and her frown just deepened. "I don't care if you're the king of England, this boy needs to rest so that he can heal."

Percy's eyes fluttered and he looked at us. One of his eyes was almost completely swollen shut, and the other one was bright red around the iris. The subconjunctival hemorrhage made him look almost demonic. I winced at first but then tried to school my expression into something more pleasant so he didn't know just how awful he looked.

"Percy, do you mind if we ask you some questions?" Thompson ignored the nurse's grunt of disgust.

"Ten minutes and that's it," she snapped, exiting the room with her shoulders stiff.

Percy stared at us with his one open eye.

"Do you know who did this to you?" Thompson asked, inching closer to the hospital bed.

"Nuuu," Percy mumbled. The word wasn't very clear because he could barely open his mouth.

"Don't try and talk." Thompson grimaced. "Just hold up one finger for yes and two for no. Okay?"

Percy attempted to nod and then winced, letting out a tight-lipped howl that could have woken the dead. He whimpered for a few moments and then fell silent. He returned to staring at us with his one good eye.

"Did you recognize your attacker?" Thompson asked.

Percy hesitated and then with a groan managed to lift two fingers.

"And you were attacked on campus near your car?"

Percy held up one finger, punctuating the movement with a moan.

"Was there anything at all about your attacker you can tell us that might help us find him or her?"

Two fingers and some more whimpers.

Thompson met my gaze. "With only yes or no answers, it's going to be hard to get any actual information out of him." I knew he was hinting I should try and read Percy in his vulnerable state. I hadn't had much luck the first time I'd met Percy, but he was weaker now. It was possible I'd be able to get inside his head.

"Yeah." I moved closer to the bed, sending out feelers. Percy's mind was fuzzy from pain meds, but I continued to probe and poke at his thoughts. The assault looped like a jumbled mess in his mind, and I winced at the brutality of the attack. I couldn't see visual details about the assault, but I was able to latch on to a few emotions: anger was the strongest. But since most victims were angry, that didn't seem that amazing. It was the simmering regret that piqued my interest the most. Percy had a tangible hunk of remorse stuck inside, eating at him.

"Why so much regret, Percy?" I spoke softly, watching him closely.

Thompson shifted but didn't say anything.

"Do you know who killed those girls?" I felt breathless. I was definitely finding Percy easier to read this time. It was probably the pain medication loosening up his mind. "You know more than you've told us, don't you, Percy?"

He held up two fingers, whimpering.

"What are you hiding?" It was so clear to me now that he knew more than he'd let on before. I narrowed my eyes and continued to probe his brain. I got a glimpse of him kissing Gloria and laughing at something she'd said. But then he suddenly blocked me. I winced when he shut me out because it was like jogging and then running smack into a wall. Grunting, I tried to access his thoughts again from another angle, but I could no longer find a way in. The way he blocked me wasn't accidental. It was intentional and calculated. He could feel me probing his mind, and he'd put up barriers.

Percy has some psychic abilities of his own.

That realization shocked me. Why hadn't I sensed that earlier? How had he shielded that from me? I held his stubborn gaze as we mentally struggled with each other. His eyes glittered feverishly, and sweat trickled down his forehead. The little bastard was pretty good.

"Is he fighting you?" Thompson sounded surprised as he watched me.

"Yes." I grunted. "Why did you hide your gift, Percy?"

He held my gaze with his one good eye, looking scared.

"If you're innocent, there's no reason to lie to us." I squinted at him, my breaths coming in quick spurts. "What are you afraid of?"

He didn't respond; he just stared at me silently, trying to hold me off.

"You should want to help us," Thompson muttered, watching the two of us. "It makes you look guilty when you hide stuff, kid."

Percy held up two fingers. "Nuuu."

"Do you know who killed those two girls?" Thompson growled.

A single tear slid down Percy's bruised cheek.

"If you're afraid of whoever it is, we can protect you." Thompson's voice was gruff.

Percy held up two fingers again as he whimpered.

A few more visions of him with Gloria, and then Valerie came to me. But none of the things I saw were violent. The memories I yanked from his mind were happy. He'd appeared fond of both girls. There was no hatred or animosity at all.

"You didn't hurt them. But you know who did." My voice was flat.

Thompson gave me a searching look, and then he took a step toward Percy. "If you know who this monster is, you need to tell us now."

"Tuu late." He started gasping and writhing around. The monitors next to his bed began buzzing and sounding alarms, and the nurse from before rushed back into the room.

"What did you do?" she snapped, leaning over Percy. She checked his pulse and then put an oxygen mask over his face. "I knew this was a bad idea. He has a partially collapsed lung. You two need to go. He's in no condition to be answering questions."

Thompson scowled. "We haven't finished talking to him."

"That's what you think." Her mouth was a hard line. "If you kill him, you can't talk to him, right? He needs to rest."

I sighed with frustration, but I had to admit, Percy did look like he was in bad shape. His lips were blue, his eyes were closed, and his breathing was ragged and weak.

"We'll be back," Thompson growled at her, then swung around and left the room, and I had no choice but to follow.

Chapter Ten

Maybe we couldn't finish questioning Percy like we'd wanted, but Thompson didn't take that lying down. The next morning he had a warrant reviewed by a prosecutor and signed by a judge. When Percy's mother opened the door, her eyes were wide as saucers as she took in me and Thompson.

Thompson showed her the warrant. "Mrs. Johnson, we have a warrant to search the premises."

She looked confused, and she adjusted the oxygen tube in her nose. "I don't understand. Why do you want to search my home?"

"As you know your son was attacked, and we're trying to figure out who would have done something like that." Thompson sounded reassuring, and he didn't mention that we actually weren't sure if Percy was a victim or a criminal yet.

"Oh, of course." She stepped back, pulling her little green oxygen tank with her. "I wanted to go see him, but I don't dare." She wheezed. "My doctor would be mad at me if I entered that germ-ridden place."

Her mind was an open book, and she was telling the truth about her health. But I found it odd she didn't seem more upset about the fact that her son was in the hospital. "So you haven't seen Percy yet?"

She coughed weakly. "No. I have a chronic lung condition. I don't dare go to the hospital." She sighed. "Also, my immune system is shit." She hobbled to a chair and sat with a loud grunt.

"We need to see Percy's room," Thompson nudged. "Could you point us to which room it is?"

"Oh, it's the one on the left." She frowned. "But Percy won't like you going through his things."

"It can't be helped." Thompson's tone was curt as he moved down the hall.

I addressed Mrs. Johnson with a little more finesse. "This could help us catch whoever attacked your son."

She nodded. "Oh, okay." She still looked worried.

"Percy won't even know we were in there. Promise."

Pressing her bony fingers to her chest, she looked relieved. "He's just so particular. I don't like to upset him. He's been extremely touchy lately."

"We'll be very careful."

"Okay."

I followed Thompson down the hallway and found him in Percy's room going through his dresser drawers. Thompson moved around the room, searching every inch, while I stood in the center of the space, trying to get a sense of who Percy Johnson really was. Something pulled me to his nightstand, and I sat on the edge of the bed and opened the top drawer.

Inside I found lube, condoms, and a stack of newspaper clippings. I frowned and pulled the clippings out. The first one was an article about a girl who'd adopted six kittens from a local shelter. I frowned, and something made me turn it over. My heart froze when I saw Steven Pine's smug face. It was a shot of him walking into court with his lawyers, and my stomach clenched at the sight of him.

I must have made a noise or something because Thompson came over. "What did you find?"

I held out the article, and he scowled.

"He's got a ton of clippings." I riffled through the other articles, and my heart began to pound as I realized every one of them was about Pine. "Shit. He seems fixated on Pine."

Thompson sat beside me. "Maybe he just found the case interesting."

"So interesting he cut out the articles? This borders on obsessive. Most people read the stories and toss them away."

He rubbed his chin. "Maybe that's why he was acting so weird at the hospital. He didn't want us to know about his obsession with Pine."

"Maybe." My stomach was in knots. "It's definitely a red flag."

"That's probably how he knew you could read his mind. The press loves to play up your psychic stuff." He peered at one of the clippings.

"Gotta sell papers." The press seemed captivated that both Pine and I were psychics. They'd fixated on that almost from the beginning. "I wish they'd focus on the fact that he slaughtered a bunch of young guys instead of the fact that he's a psychic. The victims should get more attention."

"I agree." He sighed, fingering a clipping. "So Percy must have known you were psychic from the first minute you met."

"He hid his ability and also that he knew about mine." I tensed my jaw. "Why? Why hide it?"

"Perhaps he felt awkward about his interest in Pine. He knows you aren't fond of Pine."

"That's an understatement." I scowled at the newspaper in his hand that showed Pine. "I knew that fucker was involved somehow. I just knew it."

He patted my thigh. "Yeah, you were right." He took the stack of newspaper clippings from me and went through them as he spoke. "But to be honest, right now, Pine's only tangible involvement is this kid's obsession with him."

I shook my head sharply. "No. There's more to it."

"Liam, don't let your emotions interfere. We need cold hard facts right now."

I scowled. "We have two dead girls who personally knew a guy infatuated with Steven Pine. That should set off your alarms too."

"It does. But being interested in serial killers isn't illegal." Thompson tossed the clippings back in the drawer. "We have no physical evidence that Percy is the killer. No witnesses. No DNA. Nothing. Those articles don't prove Percy is a murderer. They just prove he's even weirder than we thought."

"We never checked the visitors log for Pine."

Thompson shrugged. "Well, even if Percy went there every day, so what?" He gestured to the clippings. "We already now know he's captivated with Pine. Unless we can tie him to the actual murders, he's just a kid who likes serial killers." He stood and gave me an uneasy look. "Not to mention he just got attacked. There's no way he could do that amount of damage to himself."

Remembering Percy's swollen face and partially collapsed lung, it did seem unlikely.

"Yeah." I got to my feet and glanced around the room. "So who would want to beat up Percy?"

"That's a tough one. If the group found out Percy had been dating Gloria and Valerie, they'd be mad, but would they actually beat him up? I don't think so. They seem to revere the guy."

"But people can put on a front."

"Of course." Thompson continued searching the room as he spoke, opening and closing drawers. "Come on, Percy. You'd make my job a lot easier if I could just find a bag of pink feathers."

I laughed gruffly. "Yeah. Throw us a bone, Percy."

We searched the room for a while longer, but other than the clippings, nothing else really stood out. When Thompson's phone rang, he answered and listened for a moment. "Okay." He nodded and then shot me a triumphant look. "Email me all that. Thanks." He hung up.

"What is it?"

"I think we need to cut this short. The clippings are helpful in telling us a little about Percy, but they don't give us enough for an arrest." He moved toward the door. "But maybe we've been focused on the wrong guy."

"Who should we be focused on?" I followed him into the hallway.

"Possibly Tim Hernandez."

"Really?"

"Yep."

"What happened?"

"Old Tim wasn't a hundred percent honest with us. I'll give you details in the car." We walked into the living room and found Percy's mom on the couch, watching *People's Court* and eating Red Vines. "We're going to take off now, Mrs. Johnson." Thompson had to raise his voice because the volume of the TV was so high.

She glanced up and pressed the Mute button on the remote. "Oh, you're leaving already?"

"Yes. Something's come up. Sorry we had to interrupt your day."

"That's okay. It was kind of nice having someone else in the house. I don't like being alone." She looked around nervously. "There are a lot of people in the world who like to prey on vulnerable people like me."

"I'm sure you'll be okay." Thompson gave her one of his warmer smiles.

She tugged her sweater tighter around her neck. "It was such a shock that Percy was attacked."

"I know. This world is scary." I held her worried gaze. I wondered if she had any idea that her son was enamored of a psychopath. That fact probably wouldn't comfort her any.

"A big strapping boy like Percy should have been able to fight off anyone who attacked him." She wrinkled her brow. "He even knows martial arts."

"They must have caught him off guard." I wasn't sure I agreed with her description of Percy as a big strapping boy.

"Sure. That must be it." She sighed, got up slowly, and followed us to the door. "Have a good day, Officers," she said breathlessly and then closed the door behind us.

Once we were on the road, I addressed Thompson. "So what exactly was that phone call about?"

"Tim wasn't anywhere near Big Bear Wednesday night."

I widened my eyes. "Really? Didn't his pastor back up his claim that he was with him in Big Bear?"

"We haven't gotten a hold of his pastor yet. We've been playing phone tag. But it doesn't really matter now what his pastor says. Tim wasn't in Big Bear when he said he was. According to cell tower records, Tim's phone pinged off a tower near the LACC Wednesday night."

I scowled. "Seriously? Do you think he's the one who attacked Percy?"

"No idea. Either way, I want to know why Tim lied to us," Thompson grumbled.

"Yeah. We tried to warn him not to lie to the police." Tim hadn't really struck me as a violent type, but something had made him lie. "For all we know, he made up that whole story about seeing Gloria and Percy together."

"Easily." Thompson sounded disgusted. "What's confusing is, you said you could read that he loved Gloria. Hard to imagine him callously strangling the girl he loved."

I shivered. "Yeah. Of course, love will make people act crazy. Aren't the prisons filled with people who'd claim they loved their victims?"

"Good point." He pulled into the police station parking lot. "I had Tracy call Tim and ask him to come in for additional questioning. She texted me that he was on his way." He parked and we made our way into the station. "Let's see how his attitude is today."

While we waited for Tim to arrive, we stopped to grab coffee from the break room. Thompson bullshitted with a few other detectives, while I played Fruit Ninja on my phone. That was how it usually went around here, since most of the detectives didn't have much to say to me. I made half of them uncomfortable because they didn't believe what I did was real, and the other half found it too weird to address.

When Tracy texted Thompson that Tim was waiting for us in one of the rooms downstairs, we made our way over to that part of the building.

Entering the dingy interview room, we found Tim looking pale and uneasy.

Thompson started talking the second we entered the room, and he didn't waste time with pleasantries. "Looks like you have some explaining to do, Tim."

Lifting his chin, Tim said, "What… what do you mean?"

Thompson sat and tossed the file he held onto the metal table. "You weren't in Big Bear Wednesday night."

The color drained from Tim's face. "Um… "

"You want to tell us the truth this time about where you were Wednesday night?" Thompson's voice was raspy, and he had a more aggressive attitude with Tim than he'd used the first time we'd interviewed him.

"Well… "

"I have to wonder why you lied about something so basic."

Tim winced. "Shouldn't I have a lawyer?"

"You're not under arrest… yet. Would you like me to arrest you so you need a lawyer?"

"No," Tim mumbled, dropping his gaze to the table.

Thompson tapped his finger on the folder. "Cell phone records have you on campus Wednesday night. So why did you lie?"

"Not for the reason you probably think." Tim's voice was hushed.

"There's no logical reason to lie to the cops if you're innocent," I said. "That was plain stupid. Did you really think we wouldn't find out?"

He shook his head, his cheeks pink now. "I wasn't thinking straight. I didn't know what to do. I was scared."

"Why?"

"Because my friend had just been brutally murdered." He scowled. "I'd followed her around spying on her, and I knew you'd see me as a fucking stalker. But I'm not. I swear. All I wanted was to keep her safe, and that's it."

"Did you beat up Percy Johnson last night?" Thompson demanded. "Maybe you wanted to pay him back for messing with the girl you liked?"

Tim bugged his eyes. "What? I didn't even know anything happened to Percy."

His shock and confusion washed over me. He was telling the truth. I turned to Thompson. "He really didn't know."

Thompson grunted, hunching his shoulders. "I'm not so sure."

"You don't really think I beat him up, do you?" He looked at me, hopefully. "I didn't hurt anybody. Not one person. You believe me, right?"

I held his gaze silently.

Thompson leaned toward him, pointing his finger angrily. "You were on campus the night Gloria died. You had a crush on her and resented that she didn't return your feelings. You had opportunity and motive."

"I didn't. I didn't. I loved Gloria." His eyes were red, and his bottom lip quivered. "I loved her, I swear. I just wanted to keep her safe."

"Why did you think she needed protecting?" Thompson asked.

"Lucy told me Gloria's boyfriend had gotten a little rough with her. I just wanted to keep an eye on her."

Lucy had told him that? Seemed like a pretty personal thing to share, especially when it wasn't her story to tell. "Why would Lucy tell you Gloria's secrets?"

"I knew something was bothering Lucy. She wears her heart on her sleeve." He sighed and wiped at his eyes. "I got it out of her finally. She was really worried about Gloria." He looked up. "Only a sick fuck chokes a girl during sex."

I had to agree.

Thompson wasn't letting him off the hook that easy. "That makes it even more likely you beat up Percy. You said you thought he was her new guy. When she died, odds were you felt like Percy needed to get payback for hurting the girl you loved."

"No. I didn't touch Percy. Like I told you guys before, I had no proof Percy was seeing her. It was just a suspicion." He winced.

"So if you were there to protect her Wednesday night, how did she end up dead?" Thompson fired his questions quickly to make it harder for Tim to have lies ready.

He hung his head, and a sob broke from his chest. "I fell asleep. I fucking fell asleep." His shoulders shook as he cried hard. Tears ran down his cheeks, and he slumped on the table. "I was in my car watching the gym because I knew she liked to meet her new boyfriend there. But it was late, and I'd been up all night studying for a test and I fell asleep. I couldn't keep my eyes open, and now she's dead."

I couldn't help but feel sorry for him. I didn't know if he was lying or not, but either way he was an emotional mess. For all I knew he was crying because he'd killed her and he regretted it. I'd seen plenty of guilty people cry real tears. Tears meant nothing other than the person was upset. But why he was upset I had no actual clue.

"You expect me to believe you were in the parking lot snoozing away while someone murdered Gloria?" Thompson's voice said he thought that was bullshit.

Sniffing and wiping his nose, Tim nodded. "That's what happened. I swear on my life. I was going to spy on Gloria, and I fell asleep."

"So what happened next? You woke up and just drove home?" Thompson squinted like he couldn't believe what he was hearing.

"I woke up and no one was around. I'd blown it." He licked his lips, still looking a tad queasy. "I got out of the car and walked to the gym, but it was locked. I tried all the doors. She wasn't there, so I went home."

Thompson was silent for a few moments, his expression dubious. "Let me see your hands."

"What?" Tim looked nonplussed.

"Let me see your knuckles."

With his face scrunched in confusion, Tim held out his hands, showing his knuckles. "Why?"

I answered for Thompson. "Because if you beat up Percy, you're probably going to have bruises or scrapes of some kind." I examined his skin, and from where I sat, it appeared unscathed.

Thompson's expression was grim. "I could charge you with obstruction, Tim."

Tim held Thompson's gaze, his eyes red. "I know. But I didn't hurt anybody. I swear on my life."

Thompson got up, kicking back his chair impatiently. "You wasted my time, and the department's time. I'm trying to catch a psychopath, and you're picking and choosing what you think I need to know."

Tim dropped his chin to his chest. "I'm sorry."

Leaving the room, Thompson spoke to the officer outside the door. "He can go, but let him sit there another half hour."

I followed Thompson down the corridor, wincing as his anger radiated off him. I didn't bother to say anything. There wasn't really much to say. I knew he wanted to punish Tim for lying, but holding Tim just because he was mad at him wouldn't help anything.

"Tim said the gym was locked, and the janitor said the building was locked the next morning. So whoever killed Gloria must have a key to the gym," he said.

"True."

"I'll have Tracy call LACC's administration office and figure out who has a key to the gym." He stopped and leaned against the wall, fatigue lines under his eyes. "God, I'm beat. This case is draining."

"They're all draining." Dealing with death day in day out made keeping a good attitude challenging. But Thompson usually didn't let the stress or grim nature of our work get to him. I wondered if something else was bothering him.

"That's the truth." He pushed off the wall and headed toward the elevator.

"We should grab lunch."

His shoulders were stiff. "I'm not hungry."

I grabbed his arm right before we got in the elevator, and I pulled him to the side. A couple of people skirted around us, giving me impatient glances. "Hey, let's go grab some food and take a breather. You're wiped and grumpy."

He gave me a surly look. "Grumpy? You think I was too hard on that kid?"

"No. Not at all. He lied to us and I see why you're pissed. But we keep running into walls, and I think you're getting discouraged."

He raked a hand through his hair. "You're damn right I'm discouraged. We've got nothing. We're not one step closer to finding this killer."

"That's not true. We're slowly separating out people who didn't do it."

His mouth tensed. "But that's not good enough." He glanced around and lowered his voice. "I know there's going to be another victim soon. I can feel it."

He was right. I could feel it too. "Which is why we need to rest and regenerate."

He sighed, dropping his gaze to mine. Some of the anger left his face as he studied me. "Fine. Where do you want to eat?"

"My place."

Pulling his brows tight, he said, "Really?"

"Don't worry. I'm not cooking."

He didn't laugh like he usually would have.

I leaned into him, using a coaxing tone. "Come on. We can grab some food on the way to my place and just relax for a few hours. The world isn't going to end if we stop working the case for a couple of hours."

He gave a slow blink. "God, it would be nice to think about something else."

I was pleased he seemed to be considering my proposal. "Exactly. We deserve a break. We can get veggie burritos from Maria Bonita's."

The elevator dinged and we stepped into the empty elevator car. "Veggie burritos?" He didn't look thrilled.

"Sure. You're always nagging me to eat healthier."

He leaned against the wall. "Yeah, you. Not me. I need steak. All manly men like me need red meat."

I was happy to see he was relaxing a little. I moved closer so that our shoulders were touching. The clean scent of his cologne made my pulse rise slightly. "I'll admit, you're a fine specimen of a man."

He licked his lips. "Maybe we should just jump straight to your place and skip picking up food."

"We could do that. I do have cereal. We could have Froot Loops for lunch. That would give us more time to… relax."

A little sensual light flickered in his dark eyes. "Yeah?"

"Sure."

"Cereal, huh?"

"Yep."

He smirked. "I thought you wanted to be healthy."

"Froot Loops are healthy."

A line appeared between his dark brows. "Is that right?"

"Oh, yes. I had nothing else to read the other morning, so I read the Froot Loops box. Froot Loops are made with whole grains." I moved around to face him, and the heat of his body excited me as I leaned in. "I'm not sure if they have antioxidants, but I do know that one serving has twenty-five percent of our daily riboflavin needs."

He slipped his hands around my waist. "I love it when you talk nutrition."

"Yeah? In that case, it also has ten percent zinc and three grams of fiber."

His lips twitched. "You're such a dirty boy."

"Grrr." I couldn't keep my face straight, and I laughed.

He grinned. "Yeah, let's go to your place."

Chapter Eleven

When we entered my house, Froot Loops were the furthest thing from my mind. The minute I closed the door, Thompson had me pressed up against it, his hungry mouth covering mine. As his hands slid down my sides, my cock warmed and hardened.

When the kiss ended, I whispered, "Yeah, we can eat later."

He cupped my cheek, his eyes brown and heated. "Let's go to your room."

I nodded, my throat too tight to speak. I led the way, but his hands never left me. He stroked and pinched my ass, nipping at the nape of my neck. Once in my room, neither of us took long to get naked. I got a condom and lube from the nightstand, and my body tingled with anticipation as I laid on my side, watching him climb on the bed. His muscles flexed beautifully beneath his smooth skin, and my gut clenched with desire.

He reclined beside me, wrapping an arm around me and tugging me closer. The heat of our bare cocks pressed together excited me, and I kissed him hard, sweeping the inside of his mouth with my tongue. Nestled in Thompson's strong arms, I felt safe. The horrible details of any case always melted away when I was in bed with him.

Having his full attention was a heady experience and something I prayed I'd never lose.

We kissed each other for a few minutes, each kiss becoming deeper and more urgent. He grabbed the lube, slicked his fingers, and then he stroked my cock from root to tip, kissing me some more. I moaned and flexed my hips, wanting him inside me more than anything. He chuckled and kept squeezing and tugging at my cock.

"Thompson," I whimpered, needing more.

"Get on your stomach." His voice rumbled deep in his chest.

I obeyed, pressing my dick against the soft bedding. He ran his hands down my shoulders, spine and buttock, massaging and kneading my tingling flesh. The slick glide of his palms over my skin had me shivering with need. His hands disappeared from me, and I heard the unmistakable sound of the condom packet being ripped open.

My heart sped up, and I sighed. "Yeah, fuck me."

He straddled my thighs, still stroking and caressing my body. He trailed his fingers down the crack of my ass, pausing to tease my hole. I moaned and he laughed, rubbing against that tight bundle of nerves. "You want me inside you?"

"You know I do," I grumbled, arching my back and trying to entice him by pushing my ass in the air.

He moved a little to give my legs the freedom to move. "Open your thighs."

I did as requested, and his slick finger pushed against my entrance. I caught my breath, excitement beating through me. He teased and plucked at me some more, and by the time he inserted two fingers into me, I was clutching the sheets and begging for it.

He worked me slow and deep, pushing his fingers in all the way up to his knuckles and pulling them out. Over and over again, he slid in and out, rubbing and teasing until my entire body was shaking with the need to be taken.

He lowered himself on me, and he parted my ass cheeks, pressing the head of his cock against my opening. "You ready?"

"Yeah," I hissed, biting the pillow.

He pushed in, and a chest-deep groan broke from his lips. "Oh, *fuck*."

I squeezed my eyes closed, adjusting to the intense pressure of him entering me. It felt so good I couldn't speak for a few minutes as I simply allowed myself to enjoy the sheer deliciousness of being taken. The friction of his cock pushing in and then out was almost too much. My eyes stung with the sheer pleasure of the moment, and I pressed back, meeting his thrusts.

"Oh, fuck, Liam." His voice was hushed as he pumped his hips back and forth.

My cock rubbed against the comforter, coaxing groans from me every few seconds. His big hands pressed on the small of my back as he fucked me deeper and deeper. He was more aggressive today. I had little doubt he needed to let out his frustrations and just feel. That was fine by me. He wasn't rough or callous; he was just assertive and taking what he needed. I liked it. I loved it when Thompson got like this.

His pace picked up, and I moved so that I could stroke myself. I was close. His hunger had me so turned on, I needed to come. I slid my hand up and down my shaft as best I could, since it was trapped under my body, and he pounded into me, his muscled thighs clamped on me. "So fucking perfect," he panted.

My balls tingled with the start of my orgasm, creeping upward along my cock. I squeezed harder, my strokes becoming more urgent. "Oh, shit. I'm close. Shit." I came hard, my body shuddering and quaking with pleasure.

He grunted and froze, his cock jerking deep inside my ass. His muscles trembled as he came, pressing into me and groaning. He gave a few staggered thrusts, breathing hard, and then he sank down onto my back. He pressed his lips to my shoulder, his breath warm against my skin. "I needed that," he said softly.

"I had a feeling." I sighed.

"You know me so well." He pulled out slowly, and he laid on his back beside me, one hand resting on my thigh.

I turned over and he pulled me against him. I put my head on his chest, snuggling closer. I inhaled, loving the clean scent of his skin. "I could smell you all day."

He lifted his head and looked at me with one brow cocked. "Is that right?"

I smiled and stroked my palm over his chest. "I'm glad we skipped straight to this part."

"Me too." He exhaled roughly. "I was kind of in my head too much. You were right, I needed to step back."

"We both did."

"Yeah." He kissed my hair, and we were quiet for a moment. Then he said, "This feels so right. Don't you think?"

"Skipping lunch?"

"Liam." His voice was chiding. "I'm being serious."

I rubbed my cheek against him. "It's pretty perfect." Sometimes it felt almost too perfect, and I was afraid the universe would never let me keep it. I didn't like sharing my pessimistic view of the world with Thompson though.

He sighed. "That's better." He stroked his fingers lightly over my hip. "Jeff called me after our little dinner with him."

I stiffened. "Oh, God. Let me guess, he begged you to dump me?"

He chuckled. "Surprisingly, no."

"That is surprising." I winced, remembering how drunk I'd been.

"Actually, he nagged me about how I need to bring you to meet the rest of the family soon."

I sat up on my elbow, my eyes wide. "No. Please, Thompson. Please don't make me do that."

He frowned. "What?"

"I'm not ready. I mean, you saw how I was. That was only one family member. Now picture that level of stress times ten when I meet your parents."

"Liam, you can't be serious."

"I am. Let's wait. I mean, it's only been two months. If we make it to six months, then maybe I can meet them." My stomach ached at the idea of that family get-together.

He narrowed his eyes. "*If* we make it six months?"

"I mean when." My face warmed. That hadn't been a subconscious message to him. I wanted to spend the rest of my days with Thompson. That slip had been about insecurities about my worthiness, and nothing more. But I could tell from his annoyed expression he wasn't going to let me off that easy.

"If you mean 'when,' then why did you say 'if'?"

"Because the idea of meeting your entire family has me hyperventilating." I swallowed hard. "I didn't do so well when I met Will's family. They never liked me. You know how I am, Thompson. I'm an acquired taste at best."

"My family isn't like Will's. We're a more openminded group."

"Will's family liked plenty of people. I happen to know for a fact Will's parents loved you. Me, not so much." I glanced up at him. "You know that's true. You were close to Will. He probably told you how much they disliked me."

"Yes, he did talk to me about it. But they didn't dislike you. They didn't know you."

"I spent many Christmases with them." Every one of them had been awkward. I'd just never been able to sync with his parents. We hadn't agreed on politics or just about any social issues. That had made things weird. I'd never understood how Will could stand hanging around people who thought our being gay was a sin. It had been difficult for me to pretend everything was fine.

"I mean they didn't understand you. You're... different."

"That was the nicest way possible to put it."

His gaze was dark. "This is real for me, Liam. I love you."

"I know." I leaned up, and we kissed softly. "And I love you."

"My family is important to me."

"Yes. I know that too." I studied him. "Why are you worrying about this so much?" Was it just the case had him overthinking every little thing?

"Because I'm thirty-two. I don't want to just date you the rest of my life." He sat up, and I did too. "I'd like us to have a direction. An endgame."

That was Thompson all over. He liked things orderly and scheduled. Well, maybe not haircuts, but the important things in life. Thompson liked to have things figured out. I actually liked that about him. It comforted me that he had plans because I knew what to expect from him. But when it came to meeting his family? I'd have preferred a more laid-back approach.

"Okay. But does this endgame need to be accomplished within the first few months of dating?"

He scowled. "Are we just dating?"

"Well, no but—"

"Because I've made it pretty clear I'm not looking for that."

"As have I." I tugged the sheets around me more. "Of course I know I have to meet your family eventually. I'm merely asking for a little more time."

He studied me in silence, different emotions fluttering over his features. Impatience. Compassion. Doubt.

Doubt?

Did he doubt us? Would he push for me to meet his family if he did? No. That didn't seem like a Thompson move. He doubted my commitment to him. I could feel that suddenly very intensely. "I'm in this for real. You don't have to worry." My voice was soft and tentative.

He took my hand, intertwining our fingers. "I've waited a long time to find this. To find you."

I nodded, a lump in my throat at his vulnerable tone.

His dark lashes hid his expression. "I like waking up with you. But I hate that sometimes I'm too beat to drive over here when I want to see you." He flicked his gaze up to mine, his fear of rejection seeping through.

I cocked my head, studying him and trying to read what had him so anxious. "What are you trying to say?" I felt breathless.

"What would you think about maybe… moving in together?"

I widened my eyes, my heart speeding up. "Really?"

His jaw tensed. "Does that scare you?"

I opened my mouth to answer, but I wasn't exactly sure how to verbalize my feelings.

"Maybe I'm moving too fast."

"Well... I... "

He let go of my hand and gave a gruff laugh. "I guess I am moving too fast."

"It's not that. I'm... I'm just surprised." Until tonight, he'd never once hinted at living together. He'd seemed perfectly happy with having his own place.

"It's probably a dumb idea." He grimaced. "Maybe it would be weird to live with anyone else other than Will."

That hadn't occurred to me. My hesitancy at living with Thompson had zero to do with Will. It had everything to do with my fear of Thompson changing his mind about us.

About me.

He got off the bed, looking uptight. "Well, I'm glad this isn't awkward." He grabbed his underwear and slipped them on. "Let's just forget I said anything."

"Thompson."

He ignored me and continued to get dressed. "Unless you really want those Froot Loops, we should get back to the station." His voice was stiff, and he avoided my gaze.

I got off the bed and put my briefs on, then moved up to him. "Thompson—"

"It's fine, Liam. I get it. There are just some things that were special, and you'll never want to do them with anyone other than Will." His voice wobbled.

I took his hand and met his wary gaze. "None of this has anything to do with Will."

"Yeah, right."

"Thompson," I growled. "I'm serious."

"It's fine. I should never have even suggested it."

"No. I'm glad you did."

He chuffed. "Obviously. I could tell by the horrified expression on your face."

"That wasn't me horrified. That was me shocked."

"Either way. You didn't jump at the suggestion, did you?"

I sighed. "Not for the reasons you think." I gnawed on my bottom lip. "I love the idea of seeing you first thing in the morning and last thing at night. That isn't the problem."

"Then why did you look like you wanted to bolt out of the room?"

I decided to be honest. I didn't want him thinking I didn't want him. That was nuts. I wanted every part of him he'd give me. "Because, I'm afraid if you don't have a place to go to get away from me, you'll start noticing how irritating I am."

"What?"

"Right now, if I annoy you, you can just spend the night at your place."

"Yeah. And how many times have I done that in the last few months?"

I shrugged.

"I think I can count how many times on one hand, and those times had nothing to do with you annoying me." He scowled. "I don't need a break from you. I enjoy you."

I searched his face. "I just don't want to lose what we have by putting too much pressure on ourselves."

"I'm not naive. I've thought about this a lot." He grimaced. "The only reason I never had a truly serious relationship before was I just didn't feel it with anyone. There were plenty of nice guys, but it just wasn't enough. I feel it with you. I have for a long time."

"Living together is huge."

"It's not like I woke up this morning and thought, 'Hey, me and Liam should move in together.' I've been thinking about it every time I have to leave you to go back to my place for anything. Even though we spend all day together working, I look forward to going home with you at night. I don't need a break from you. I don't need a place to escape to. I just need you."

My eyes stung at his sincerity. "Shit, Thompson. I didn't know you were a romantic." I laughed gruffly.

He smirked. "I can pull it out when I need to."

"Is the moving in together why you want me to meet your family?"

"Not exactly. I want to live together either way. I guess I simply want the people I love to all know each other."

"Even if they don't like me?"

"Jeff warmed up to you faster than I thought he would."

I grimaced. "I don't think he exactly warmed up to me. I think he felt sorry for me because I was such a train wreck."

He grinned. "We'll take what we can get."

"So if your entire family thinks I'm weird, and they all believe you're making a horrible mistake by being with me, that's no problem for you?" I squinted disbelievingly.

"I like who you are. My family doesn't make my decisions for me."

My body was tense. "I'm all for living together. But the family meeting will have to wait." I watched him uneasily, wondering if that would be a deal breaker.

But he didn't look upset. He widened his eyes, looking excited. "Really? You want to move in with me?"

"Yes." I shrugged. "I hate it when you aren't here."

He hugged me, squeezing me so tight it was difficult to breathe. "That's great." His energy became more guarded as he said softly, "I guess the next question would be, do you move in with me… or do I move in with you?"

I knew instinctively he didn't want to live in the home I'd shared with Will. He was trying to hide it from me, but his reticence came through to me. I understood his feelings, since he already had an insecurity where Will was concerned. But there was a certain melancholy to the idea of leaving behind the home Will and I had made together. Poignant memories were present in things as simple as the paint colors we'd chosen, and sometimes argued over. We'd planted hydrangeas in the backyard and put in new kitchen cabinets. Will was still very much alive for me in this house, and that was probably the main reason Thompson preferred to live somewhere else.

"We'll have to think about that." I wasn't ready to decide right that minute. Not because I didn't love Thompson enough. That was most definitely not the problem. But it was going to hurt leaving all my memories of this place and William behind. I wasn't ready to face that just yet.

"No rush." He kissed my hair and released me. "We should head back."

"Yeah."

He left the room, and I stood there for a few minutes, feeling strangely emotional. But then I followed him out of the house. There were more important things to focus on right now other than my love life.

S.C. Wynne

Chapter Twelve

Any time we tried to arrange another interview with Percy in the hospital, we were thwarted by that bossy nurse. So instead we spent the next four days interviewing as many students as we could, trying to rule out everyone possible. There were no new murders during that time, which made Thompson even more convinced Percy was our man. He figured if no one died while Percy was incapacitated, that was telling.

I didn't exactly disagree with him, but I was concerned that I couldn't sense any homicidal tendencies off the kid. The only things I'd found in Percy's memories were affectionate moments with both Gloria and Valerie. If he was the killer, it was odd that I would only glimpse those happy times and wouldn't also have stumbled upon the memories of the murders.

Another frustration was we still couldn't find any connection between Shalondra and the other two homicides. The only indicator that her death was linked to the other two was that I'd seen her murder, and then her spirit had come to me. Not exactly something that could hold up in a court of law. We needed physical evidence to link her to the others.

Even though we already knew Percy was a fan of Steven Pine, we went ahead and checked the jail's visitor logs for any visits by Percy. We didn't find any. But we did discover that Percy and Pine had corresponded through the mail. Of course, even with that information, that didn't mean we could just go arrest Percy for being a creep. It was just one more string of information that we weren't sure what to do with. We suspected Percy was connected to the murders somehow. But we needed to find something that put him at one of the actual crime scenes before we could arrest him.

When Thompson finally got the call that Percy had been released from the hospital, his eyes lit up. He stood and grabbed his jacket from the back of his chair. "Let's go."

I frowned, looking up at him. "Where?"

"We're going to have a little 'knock and talk' with Percy."

A "knock and talk" was where a police officer knocked on someone's door and tried to get them to talk to them. Cops used it a lot when they didn't have enough evidence for an arrest warrant, but they really, really wanted to talk to someone. Many people didn't understand they didn't have to talk to the cops just because they showed up at their door. So this tactic could sometimes yield great results. I just hoped Percy didn't know too much about the law.

When we arrived at Percy's home and Thompson knocked on the door, there was no answer. That didn't seem to sit well with Thompson, and he scowled and knocked some more.

"It's weird the mom isn't at least answering the door," I said softly. "She implied she doesn't go out much because of her health."

"Yeah." Thompson nodded. "And I know Percy's home. His car is in the driveway."

"Maybe they're napping?"

Thompson pulled his brows together. "Both of them at the same time?"

I laughed. "Well, I don't mean in the same bed."

He sighed and banged on the door again, calling out, "This is Homicide Detective Kimball Thompson. If you're home Percy, I'd love to talk to you."

No answer.

I stepped off the porch and tiptoed carefully through the flower bed, trying not to crush the yellow lilies planted there. I wanted to see if I could peek in one of the windows along the front of the house. There were brown ruffled curtains blocking my view, but I moved around until I found a few cracks between the fabric. Ignoring the dead flies in the windowsill, I peered through the brown, dusty material.

At first I couldn't see anything, but as my eyes adjusted to the darker interior of the home, I saw Mrs. Johnson on the couch. She and Percy faced each other as he sat across from her. Percy was talking, and Mrs. Johnson looked uneasy. When Thompson banged on the door again, she jumped and pressed her hand to her chest.

"They're both in the living room," I whispered to Thompson.

"Seriously? Do they not hear me knocking?"

"I think they hear you."

He scowled and pounded on the door even harder. "Percy, I need to ask you a few more questions."

Neither Percy nor his mother budged. I continued to watch them, wondering why Mrs. Johnson looked so unsettled. I'd have thought she'd be thrilled that her son was home and well. When Percy turned his head suddenly toward me, I ducked down and held my breath. I waited a few seconds, and then I crept back toward Thompson.

"I think he saw me." I laughed.

"Why the hell aren't they answering the door?" Thompson looked puzzled.

"Maybe he knows he doesn't have to."

Thompson stepped back from the door, his jaw clenched. "What is this guy hiding?"

"A lot I think."

The sound of the door unlocking had me and Thompson stiffening. When the door opened, Percy stood there looking bruised and wary. The swelling had gone down, but one side of his face was still purple and mottled. "Detective Thompson?"

I had to hand it to Thompson, he didn't miss a beat the minute the door opened. "Would you mind if we came inside to talk?" Thompson sounded confident, but we both knew Percy didn't have to let us in without a warrant.

"I'm not sure." Percy frowned.

"You want to help us solve this case, right?" Thompson prodded. "We still need to catch whoever attacked you too."

"We just want to ask you a few things. It would be really helpful to talk with you again," I said.

Percy's gaze moved to me almost as if he hadn't realized I was standing there. Something seemed to change in his expression the second his gaze lit on me. "Come in." His eyes never left me as he stood aside and waved us in.

Mrs. Johnson stayed seated. "Oh, it's so nice to see you boys again." She almost sounded as if we were all ten and we'd dropped by for a game of kickball with her son. "Do you have another warrant to search the house?"

Percy frowned, giving her a confused glance. "Another warrant?"

Thompson cleared his throat. "While you were laid up in the hospital, we searched your room." He watched Percy closely.

"Really?" Percy's face flushed.

"Yep," Thompson said quietly.

Percy shifted uneasily. "Find anything interesting?"

"Disturbing might be a better word," I said.

Percy's glance flicked to his mother. "Would you mind, Mother? I'd like to talk to with Detective Thompson in private."

"I won't interrupt."

Grimacing, Percy said, "I'd rather it was a private conversation. You should go lie down. It's time for your nap anyway."

"But I'm not tired." She frowned.

He moved closer to her. "You need your rest. Your doctor said you should take a nap in the afternoon, remember?"

She pouted. "I won't be able to sleep. I'm too wound up."

Percy's jaw tensed. "Go lie down, mother. The things I need to discuss with Detective Thompson might upset you."

"Oh." She stood, looking flustered. "I don't want to hear anything bad. I'll just go rest like you suggested, Percy." She inched around her son giving me a weak smile. "Percy takes such wonderful care of me."

He didn't say anything, just watched her make her way past us.

"I'll be in my room if you need me," she wheezed, tugging her oxygen tank after her down the hall.

Once her door closed, Percy faced us. "If you searched my room, I assume you saw my newspaper clippings." It wasn't a question.

"We did," Thompson responded.

"I'm sure you think the worst." He sighed.

"We're a little concerned that you seem obsessed with Steven Pine." Thompson pulled his pad and pen from his pocket. "He's a sick man."

"He's a complicated man." Percy lifted his chin.

Percy's stubborn tone annoyed me. Anyone who thought Pine was anything other than a twisted psycho was an asshole in my book. "We also know you and Steven Pine are pen pals."

Percy winced. "I don't expect you to understand, but to me, he's a fascinating person."

"Right. Fascinating." My voice was hard. "He's a heartless butcherer."

"Granted, he has impulse-control issues." Percy nodded.

I huffed. "He's nuts."

"I don't think so. I think he's misunderstood."

I widened my eyes. "So… you see nothing wrong with him murdering five young men and trying to kill me?"

"Naturally you're taking that personally." Percy grimaced. "But when you talk to him, you see that he had a reason. Or at least… he felt he did."

"He thinks he's an angel." My voice was flat. "He's more like a devil."

"Given your history with him, I can see we'll never see eye to eye on this." Percy crossed his arms.

"You've got that right," I snapped.

"But whether we agree or not, it's not illegal to talk to him." Percy lifted his chin. "I realize most people won't see what I do in Steven, but it's not against the law to correspond with him."

"No. You're right. But it definitely makes me wonder about what kind of a person you are, Percy." It took effort to keep my voice emotionless. "He's a murderer. What do you have in common with him?"

He squinted at me. "I correspond with him because I'm interested in his psychic ability."

"That's another thing," Thompson interjected. "Why didn't you tell us you had psychic abilities when you first met us?"

"He didn't just not tell us," I said. "He purposely hid it."

Percy twisted his lips, looking uncomfortable. "I didn't see what it had to do with the case."

"You didn't see how being psychic and a pen pal with a serial killer might be of interest to us?" I laughed sardonically. "I'm not buying it."

"People treat me differently when they know about my… gift." He touched his bruised cheek absentmindedly. "Besides, my abilities aren't that great."

"They're respectable." He'd definitely been able to block me well enough. "You showed that that night at the hospital."

"Well, I didn't appreciate you trying to get inside my head when I was so vulnerable. I was in a lot of pain and weak from being attacked." He looked annoyed.

"If you'd just been honest with us about stuff from the beginning, I wouldn't have needed to try that route."

Thompson perked up. "That reminds me, Percy, have you been able to recall any details about who attacked you?"

Percy's jaw clenched and he dropped his gaze. "I'm afraid not."

"Nothing at all?" Thompson nudged. "Maybe his weight or height?"

"No. Sorry. It all happened so fast." His voice was clipped.

"Hmmm." Thompson didn't look convinced.

"You seem to have recovered remarkably well," I interjected. Other than the big purple bruises on one side of his face, he didn't seem to be in pain.

"I have some pain meds. But I don't like to use them. Sometimes you just have to push through," Percy said softly. He shifted, and a necklace around his neck made a noise.

The distinctive sound made my ears prick, and when I met Thompson's alert gaze, I knew he'd heard it too.

I don't know his real name, but she called him Clinky.

"So was that what you wanted to talk to me about? Those newspaper clippings?" Percy took a step toward the door. "Cuz... I'm pretty tired. I should probably rest."

Nice try, Percy.

"Come on, Percy. You know there's more to discuss," Thompson said.

His face tensed. "Like what?"

Thompson barely paused. "Were you aware some of the members of your Always Listening group suspected you were seeing both Gloria and Valerie romantically?"

Percy blanched. "What?"

"They thought you were dating Gloria and Valerie." Thompson kept his face blank.

"No. I... I didn't allow that stuff in my group."

I gave him a doubting look. "You just didn't let anyone else date. But Tim Hernandez saw you with Gloria." I fudged the truth a little to see if he'd give us something.

He licked his lips, looking embarrassed. "Tim said that?"

"Yep," I lied.

Wincing, he said, "You have to understand, they came on to me. Girls never came on to me before I started that group."

Gotcha.

"So you were sleeping with both of them?" Thompson asked.

"I liked them. It wasn't just sex. I connected with them personally as well." His face was red. "But when all of a sudden two hot girls hit on me, why would I say no?"

Thompson didn't look sympathetic. "You have a key to the gym, don't you, Percy?"

Percy sat down on the arm of the couch as if his legs had given out. "Yes," he said softly. "Why?"

"Whoever murdered Gloria had a key," Thompson said.

Percy widened his eyes. "Wait a minute —"

"Why would you have a key?" I asked.

"Because sometimes we'd have our meeting in there. My Always Listening group shares a... a classroom with the chess club, and sometimes our meetings would be on the same night. I talked the administration into letting me use the gym a couple of times a month."

"There are a lot of things that are starting to look really bad for you, Percy." Thompson stepped closer to the boy. "You had intimate relationships with both victims, and you've lied about numerous things."

"Are you going to arrest me?" Percy looked terrified, and he fingered his necklace.

"I definitely think you're a person of interest." Thompson's voice was gruff.

Percy stood and backed away from us. "You're making a big mistake." He looked sweaty, and his eyes darted around the room. "A huge mistake."

"In what way?" Thompson asked.

"He's not going to just let you arrest me."

"Who?" I frowned.

"We're way too close to the endgame now." He gave a stiff smile. "I didn't know what was going to happen. But I couldn't say no. I didn't know ahead of time what would happen. I don't think I should be held responsible." He looked muddled. "But he has work to do, and I couldn't stand in the way of that just because I was fond of them."

"You didn't know what was going to happen?" I asked. He wasn't making much sense, and he looked like he didn't feel well.

"I truly did like those girls. But it's not about me. It's not about this life."

I frowned. "What are you talking about?"

"The big picture."

I met Thompson's confused gaze. "Are you following this?"

"Not really," Thompson said.

Percy pressed a hand to his head, and he winced. "Oh, God. Now look what you've done."

I had to admit, he didn't seem to be faking. He truly looked freaked-out. "Percy, we're just talking. Just be open with us."

"No. No. He knows what this is leading to. He's not going to stand for it." His eyes widened. "Liam, you should probably run."

I gave a confused laugh. "What?"

"You are not his favorite person. To put it mildly." His voice wobbled, and he stumbled sideways, catching himself on the wall. "He knew you'd work this case, and he knew he'd get his chance at you again. This has all happened just as he predicted."

"Why is he talking in third person? Is he having a psychotic break?" Thompson looked bewildered as he glanced at me.

"Possibly."

Percy scowled at me. "You think I'm crazy?"

"I… um…" I wasn't sure how to respond.

"You just don't get it. He really is a genius, and his powers are awe-inspiring," Percy mumbled. "But I was just the conduit. I can't be blamed for what happened. Not really." He frowned. "Will I be blamed? People are so shortsighted."

"Look, why don't you let us take you to the ER?" Thompson moved toward Percy.

Percy shuddered and bugged his eyes. "Don't say I didn't warn you!"

Chills went through me at the raw panic in his voice. He crumpled to his knees and seemed to convulse. Thompson moved toward him but then stopped, looking unsure of what to do. Percy groaned and his muscles clenched and shook as he cried out as if in pain. But then he fell silent, and the only sound in the room was his ragged breathing.

Thompson met my gaze questioningly, and I shrugged, completely confused by what was happening with Percy. I wasn't sure if we should call 911 or if he was putting on some sort of nutty show for us.

Percy exhaled and stretched his arms out to his side, still in a kneeling position. "Wow." His voice was deeper than before. "That was intense."

"What are you playing at?" Thompson growled.

Percy looked up at Thompson, and something about his face looked different. Older. Meaner. Familiar. Valerie's words came back to me:

His face was different. Not the same. Not the same.

I shivered at the menacing gleam hidden in the depths of Percy's eyes. I narrowed my eyes, searching the boy's face. His skin seemed pulled tighter over his angular features, and his face didn't look quite right. "Percy?"

He gave a tight-lipped smile. "Wrong." That one-word answer was followed by a giggle that sent fear jolting through me. "Did you miss me, Liam?"

S.C. Wynne

Chapter Thirteen

I clamped my jaw tight as my heart banged against my ribs. Fear and disbelief buzzed through me as my numb brain grappled with what was happening. Everything in me screamed that my hunch was preposterous. "Thompson."

"I see it." Thompson's voice was hard.

"That isn't possible," I muttered. "It's physically impossible." I stared at Percy, trying to reject what my eyes clearly saw. It was almost as if Steven Pine's face was layered over Percy's. Even the way he stood was different, and yet terrifyingly familiar.

Pine sighed. "I know this is a shock, boys. But I did warn you when we last met that wasn't the end of things."

"There's no fucking way," I growled.

Snapping his fingers, Pine hissed, "Wake up and smell the coffee, Liam. This is real, and you're not going to like how it ends."

Thompson gave a sharp intake of breath and lunged toward Pine. Before he could reach him though, Pine stuck his arm out, and Thompson gave a grunt and fell backward as if someone had punched him. His body slammed into the couch, and the large piece of furniture slid across the wooden floor, knocking into the TV stand and sending the TV crashing to the floor.

Thompson lay motionless on the floor, and panic gripped me as I moved toward him. I was inches from Thompson when something clenched on my throat. I gasped for air as a seemingly invisible grip squeezed my windpipe. I fell to my knees, wheezing for air like a hooked trout.

Mrs. Johnson came out of her bedroom with her eyes wide. "What's going on?" The squeak of the oxygen tank's little wheels was barely discernible above the roaring in my ears. "Percy. What's happening?"

The grip on my throat stopped suddenly, and Pine faced her. "Everything is fine. You should go back in your room." The voice that came from Percy's lips was different, and Mrs. Johnson seemed to notice.

"You're back?" Her usually amiable expression changed into an angry one. "I've told you, I don't want you here."

Did she know about Pine? I'd never gotten even a hint of that off her. But right then, my main concern was Thompson. Since she had Pine distracted, I inched toward Thompson, feeling sick to my stomach because he was so still and pale. Once I reached him, I felt for his pulse. When the even beat met my touch, I slumped with relief.

Thank God.

Mrs. Johnson was in front of Pine, wagging her finger in his face. "We've talked about this. You can't just keep changing into different people, Percy. Everyone will think you're crazy."

Pine exhaled impatiently. "I really don't have time for this right now, Alma."

She scowled at his use of her first name and glanced over at me and Thompson. "What did you do? Assaulting a police officer will get you arrested. I don't understand what's gotten into you lately. You're coming in at all hours and staying locked in your bedroom. I think we need to see a specialist, Percy. This can't go on."

Pine rolled his eyes, a disgusted look on his face. "Seriously, I do not have time for you right now, old woman."

She gasped. "Excuse me?"

He leaned toward her and took hold of her shoulders. "Okay. That's enough. Time to go night night." He touched her head, and she widened her eyes and then slumped. He shook his head. "The old bat thinks Percy is schizophrenic." He huffed as he dragged the older woman to the couch. He hoisted her up on the sofa, patting her head as he straightened. "See, I'm not completely heartless. I won't make Percy kill his own mom."

I silently watched him, fear eating at my gut. If this was actually Pine, I already knew his powers were way stronger than mine. Trying to take him on head-to-head wasn't going to work.

What do I mean if this is Pine? How can it be Pine? How?

He faced me looking smug. "I'm sure this is horribly confusing for you, Liam."

I didn't speak.

He sighed. "It's amazing you and Thompson solve any cases. I mean, this is the second time we've worked together, and you guys were as clueless as last time."

"And you're as psychotic as ever."

He curled his lip. "God, you're a mouthy little fucker. You never give me the respect I deserve. I'm getting sick of that."

"I can't even believe this is happening."

"Well, you should. I'm right here in front of you." He glanced at Thompson. "You know what I can't believe? That you two are still together. Can you explain to me what the attraction is between you two? You're both so different."

The moment felt surreal enough without him weighing in on my love life. I didn't respond to him. I was still trying to get my head around the fact that somehow Steven Pine had taken over Percy's body, and I was probably about to die.

He smirked. "No probably about it. You're going to die." He sighed. "I'll admit, on one hand that's kind of too bad."

"Yeah, I'm sure you'll cry yourself to sleep every night."

"I'm serious. Sure, your powers are pathetic compared to mine, but you're much stronger than the average psychic. It's been kind of fun toying with you. At least you challenge me a little."

I simply glared at him.

He laughed. "I thought about you a lot the last few months. I had a ton of unresolved anger toward you, Liam. You really fucked up my work for a while."

"Good," I growled.

He pressed his lips together, anger sparking in his eyes. "Then Percy reached out to me. Oh, my Lord, I couldn't believe my luck when Percy reached out to me." He cackled. "God knew I still had so much work to accomplish, and he sent me a loyal disciple."

As much as I hated him, I was fascinated with how he'd accomplished this most recent psychic trick. Even as I struggled to accept it was happening, I was morbidly intrigued. "I've never heard of anyone being able to possess another person from a distance."

"I'm not like anyone else."

I had to grudgingly agree. "So enlighten me. Brag a little."

He squinted at me. "You're probably just stalling, but that's okay. I deserve to brag."

"How could you possibly hijack Percy's body like this?" I scanned his twisted face.

"What's happening to your body while you're here? Did you switch places with Percy? Is he in your body?"

He snorted. "Lord no. He can't transport himself. I have to share his body. It's crowded, but I find Percy is submissive enough I can do what I need to do."

"You mean like murder the girls he had feelings for?" My voice was hard.

"Yeah." He sighed. "He really did like them too. And they were so fucking confused because they really trusted old Percy." He shrugged. "But all these depressing souls just take up space. They need to be cleansed and gotten rid of to make way for better souls."

I scowled. "You seriously think you're doing God's work?"

His face tensed. "How many times do I have to tell you I'm an angel? Angels killed plenty of people in the bible. Not sure why you think we're sweet and loving. We do what needs doing."

I ignored his snide tone. "I still don't get how you move from body to body."

He tugged his necklace from his shirt. "This has a receptacle inside it."

I frowned.

"It's very tiny. But it doesn't need to hold much."

"Much what?"

"Blood." His face was flushed and his eyes bright, as if he could barely control himself from blurting everything out. "The blood acts as a conductor. I can move between Percy and my body. It's an insane rush. You should try it."

"No, thanks."

He snorted. "You're so judgmental."

"So Percy has a necklace. How does that get you inside his body?"

"I have one of these too."

I scowled. "Bullshit. They don't allow anything other than wedding rings in jail."

His smile was pompous. "They wouldn't deny a man his faith."

"Meaning what?"

"The justice system makes allowances for some pieces of jewelry if they're religious in nature. It just took bribing the right guard and I had my necklace."

"I still don't get how that connects you to Percy."

"They both have blood in them. The same blood." His tone was lecturing. "It links Percy to me."

A chill went through me. "Whose blood?"

"Does it matter? We just needed fresh blood." He shrugged. "It was some hooker Percy found."

I widened my eyes. *Shalondra?* "What was her name?"

He scrunched his face impatiently. "How the fuck would I know? It was just some bitch who nobody would miss. As usual you're getting caught up in the unimportant details."

Thompson stirred, and groaning, he sat up. His mouth was a grim line as he met my gaze. "You okay?" he sounded groggy as he flicked his uneasy gaze to Pine.

I opened my mouth, but I had no idea how to respond.

Pine sighed. "Awww. He's worried about you, Liam." He smirked.

Thompson had a deep line between his eyes. "Is this really happening? Is he actually... is he..." He shook his head.

"Yes." I swallowed hard.

"How?"

"Oh, we've been over that while you were snoozing." Pine smirked. "I used the blood of a dead hooker to move between Percy and me."

"What?" Thompson looked suitably confused as he pressed his fingers to his head.

"It's a long story," I said gruffly. "But I finally know how Shalondra figures in."

Thompson just frowned.

Pine studied me as he spoke. "Percy didn' really have a killer's instinct. But of course, he hac to do the first murder in order for us to link up." He lifted one brow. "Poor kid puked and had nightmares for a month. But he did it. I had to give him credit for following through."

"Why kill those young girls?" Thompson's voice was hoarse.

"They didn't deserve to live. Life is a gift, and they tried to throw it away. They needed to be cut out like cancer."

"They were in a support group. Obviously they wanted to live," Thompson said gruffly.

"Did they? I'm not so sure."

"What was the point of the questions?" I asked.

His smile was chilling. "The only question I actually cared about was the fate one. I mean, if they believed in fate, then meeting me was a part of that plan, right?"

"What if they'd said they didn't believe in fate?" Thompson shifted his position, wincing slightly.

"I believe in fate," Pine snapped. "That's good enough."

"So then our catching you the first time was fate?" I spoke softly.

Pine's expression flickered. "That was a fluke."

"Or maybe God wants you stopped because you're a sick fuck," I grumbled.

He screwed up his face in anger, and he took a step toward me. "You never show me the respect I deserve, Liam. Your insolence is tiring."

The choking pressure from earlier returned to my throat, and I struggled to breathe while trying not to panic. I grabbed my neck, gagging for oxygen as my eyes watered.

"I can kill you so easily. I could snap your neck in two seconds. But still you pick at me and pick at me. Why? Why do you think that's okay?"

"Leave him alone," growled Thompson.

"Why? We're just delaying the inevitable." Pine's light eyes were malevolent.

"Who attacked you?" Thompson asked abruptly.

Pine's gaze flickered, and he looked at Thompson impatiently. "What?"

"Who beat you up?"

He gave a tight smile and released his hold on my throat. I coughed and held my throbbing neck as he answered. "Oh, that was me." He giggled.

Thompson scowled. "You beat... yourself up?"

"I had to do something. You guys were honing in on Percy, and we needed him to be a victim, not a suspect." He grimaced. "But I guess it didn't work because you showed up here looking to arrest Percy."

"Too many unanswered questions," Thompson said.

"I'll keep that in mind for next time." Pine smirked at me and then snapped his gaze to Thompson and growled, "Touch your gun and I'll break Liam's neck."

Thompson froze, and his face flushed. He moved his hand away from his waistband where I knew he kept his gun. His jaw was tight and his eyes angry. "Can't blame a guy for trying."

"It's useless. Maybe even pathetic since I know what you're going to do before you do it."

I felt demoralized as I met Thompson's concerned gaze. I was out of ideas. I wasn't psychically strong enough to fight Pine, and while Thompson could probably physically take Pine, he'd never get the chance. He'd never be able to get close enough to do any damage. I held Thompson's dark eyes, feeling brokenhearted. I loved him so much. I couldn't believe this was how it ended for us. It was so fucking unfair.

When Shalondra materialized behind Pine, I didn't believe my eyes for a second. Her ebony skin was ashen, and her black eyes glittered with anger. My heart banged against my ribs as she held my gaze. I didn't understand how she could reappear, but I wanted to believe maybe I could use it to save us. My throat was tight, but I forced myself to speak.

"You know, Pine, that hooker you thought no one would miss had a name." My voice was raspy. I wasn't sure why Shalondra was here. Had she heard what he'd said? Was she just randomly appearing again, like she'd done before? "She had a life, and you took it from her."

Thompson glanced over at me confused.

"What?" Pine looked annoyed.

"Her name was Shalondra."

"Who gives a fuck?" Pine snapped.

I swallowed hard. "I do. I give a fuck."

Shalondra cocked her head as she watched me.

"She didn't deserve to die like that." I met Thompson's puzzled gaze, praying he'd be ready to act if the opportunity presented itself. "You… you shouldn't have killed her, Pine."

"What are you rattling on about a dead whore for?"

"You murdered her in cold blood."

Nodding, Shalondra said, "Yeah. I didn't deserve to die, motherfucker."

Pine stiffened and looked around. From his reaction, I suspected he'd heard her, but he didn't seem to see her, even though she was only inches from him. He gave me an angry look. "What the hell are you playing at?"

"Nothing." My voice was hushed. "I just know Shalondra would want you to pay for what you did to her."

"Yeah… someone needs to pay." Her eyes were wide as she stared at the back of Pine's head.

Pine shivered and glanced over his shoulder quickly. "Nice try, Liam." He took a step toward me, and the choking sensation was back.

I gasped as the pressure increased on my windpipe. Thompson looked horrified, and he grabbed my arm. His panic was palpable, but when he reached for his gun again, Pine kicked him off balance, sending him sprawling onto his back.

Behind Pine, Shalondra hovered, her face dark and furious. She waved her arm and a picture flew off the mantel straight toward Pine's head. He batted it away, looking startled. The grip on my throat tightened, and I clawed at my neck futilely. Pine knelt beside me, his eyes filled with hate. "Feel that? That's me proving once and for all that you're nothing compared to me," he growled. His anger lashed against me as I began to lose consciousness.

"I didn't deserve to die, motherfucker," Shalondra hissed as she sent a lamp crashing toward Pine.

He ignored the projectiles she sent his way and squeezed harder. "Sorry, bitch, I'm not sure who you are, but when he dies you're gone." He shoved me to the ground, using his body weight to hold me down as he strangled me.

As I began to fade away, the shiny glint of something swinging back and forth in front of my blurry eyes caught my attention. Back and forth, back and forth, the silver pendant taunted me only inches from my face.

"Get off of him!" Thompson again tried to pull his gun, but Pine sent Thompson flying in the opposite direction.

I put everything I had left into lifting my arm. My muscles burned and didn't want to obey, but I concentrated hard, forcing my aching body to respond. With a grunt, I made a desperate swipe at the glistening necklace. Miraculously, my fingers looped around the silver chain, and I yanked with all my might.

The necklace snapped free and dangled in my clasped hand. Pine screamed and convulsed, his face contorted in pain and rage. "You fucker. *You little fucker.* You're ruining everything!" Spittle hit my face as he growled and struggled to stay in Percy's body.

He let go of my throat, and I wheezed and choked oxygen back into my stinging lungs. Thompson was over me now, sliding his arm under my shoulders and pulling me against his chest. "Liam, shit. Are you okay?" His voice was hoarse against my ear.

I couldn't talk. My throat was raw and painful, and I still gasped for air. The skin of my neck throbbed where Pine's fingers had been.

Once the necklace was off Percy's neck, Pine seemed to evaporate. Percy was crumpled in a heap on the floor, pale and barely breathing. Shalondra was still there, shimmering translucently behind Thompson. Her expression was emotionless, and her earlier anger seemed to have disappeared.

Thompson kissed my forehead, his eyes red and worried. "He's gone. You're okay. You're okay, right, Liam?" His fear washed over me like a tsunami as he dialed 911 on his phone. He spoke curtly into his cell, and his gaze never left me.

Once I could stop struggling so hard for oxygen, I slowly sat up. Thompson kept his hand on my shoulder, as if afraid to let go of me. I touched my tender neck, wincing at how painful it was. "They need to take away Pine's necklace immediately," I whispered hoarsely.

"Yeah." Thompson nodded and made another call.

Shalondra stayed near us until the cops arrived, and then she slowly faded away. Thompson insisted the paramedics checked me out before Percy. I felt a little guilty about that, but Thompson wasn't in the mood to listen. Other than extreme bruising, the paramedics thought I'd be fine. Although they did suggest I see my regular GP to get an X-ray to rule out any permanent damage that couldn't be detected visually.

When Percy came to, he looked completely confused. Thompson arrested him and read him his rights. Percy's mother sniffled and wheezed as the cops took her son away. I felt bad for her. She had no idea what was happening, and she was still under the impression that Percy was schizophrenic. I didn't have the heart, or the energy, to tell her otherwise. She probably wouldn't have believed me anyhow.

I sat on the front porch, letting the warm afternoon sun heat my chilled body, as Thompson spoke with the other detectives and cops who were on the scene. Eventually he came outside, and we went to his car.

Once inside, he faced me, his features tense. "There has to be a way to control Steven Pine. He's not going to stop until he eventually kills you." His voice was harsh. "Obviously, that's not okay with me."

"I have no answers. But I think you're right. So long as he's alive, he's a threat." Hell, knowing Pine, even dead he'd try and get to me.

Thompson raked a shaky hand through his hair. "I've told everybody who'll listen he's not to have any jewelry of any kind. But he'll probably just try and find another way."

I touched his hand that rested on the shift. "We've gone head-to-head twice, and so far he's 0 for 2. Have a little faith," I whispered, curling my fingers into his and loving the firm heat of his skin. "We're the good guys."

His mouth twitched in a grudging smile. "You think the good guys always win?"

"I have to. The alternative is too bleak." I spoke quietly, favoring my sore throat.

"How the hell do we even prove any of this?" He exhaled, squeezing my hand.

"I don't know. Maybe we can't. It's not like we can bring Shalondra in for questioning."

"And Percy will go down for attacking everybody while Pine gets away scot-free."

"It's unbelievable. But unavoidable. No one will accept what we just witnessed. The best we can do is make sure our first case sticks."

"Jesus. I feel powerless."

"Yeah. Because we are. But for now he's in jail." I rested my head against the seat. "Shalondra kind of saved us today."

He studied me. "I had no idea she was even there."

"Yeah. Pine could hear her, but he couldn't see her." I felt grateful to Shalondra, even though she hadn't even known how helpful she was. She'd simply shown up at the right time, and her distraction had been what saved us.

"I was thinking… we should have a funeral for her."

"Shalondra?"

I nodded. "It's not right that she was just tossed aside and nobody cared. She deserves a little service and some respect."

He grimaced. "That's a little unorthodox."

I laughed. "Something tells me that would suit Shalondra just fine."

He started the car. "I'm taking you home, and then I'm heading in to write up my report."

"I don't want to go home without you."

"Liam, you look like you're ready to fall down. Your throat must be killing you."

"I'm going to the station with you, Thompson." I clenched my jaw. After what we'd just gone through, I wasn't leaving his side.

He exhaled. "Okay. I want you near me anyway."

I smiled and closed my eyes. "That's better."

Epilogue

"Bureaucratic red tape," I grumbled. Thompson had brought me to our favorite sushi restaurant to celebrate my thirtieth birthday. I sipped my ice tea, feeling grumpy. "Why would they care if we gave Shalondra a funeral?"

"Because the people in charge don't feel enough time has passed to allow family members to come forward to claim the body."

"Seriously?"

"Two months isn't enough time." He sipped his beer, letting out a long sigh.

"Meanwhile she's in a freezer."

"If no one comes forward soon, they'll cremate her. Then eventually she'll be buried in a mass grave along with all the other unclaimed people this year."

"Seems wrong."

"I know. Do you think she'll be back to visit you?"

"Maybe. I get the feeling Shalondra's spirit will do what she wants."

The waitress set our yellowtail and spicy crab rolls on the table with a smile. Her feet were killing her, and she couldn't wait for her shift to be over, but I appreciated that she hid that from us.

Once she'd left, Thompson held up his beer. "Happy birthday, Liam."

"Thanks." I sighed and bumped my glass against his. "Sorry I'm so obsessed with this whole Shalondra thing."

"Well, she did help save our lives. I understand."

I popped one of the yellowtail into my mouth, sighing at how fresh the fish was. I swallowed and caught Thompson smiling at me. "What?" I lifted one brow.

He shrugged. "I'm just happy."

My chest tightened at the warmth in his eyes. "Yeah?"

"Definitely."

"I'm happy too." I thought about our run-in with Pine a few days ago. "For a moment there, I didn't think we had a future anymore."

His expression became more serious. "You mean because of Pine?"

"Yes." I touched my throat. The skin was still bruised and tender, and I wore a high collar so no one noticed.

"Pine is on lockdown until his trial, and all signs point to him going away for a long time." His voice was gruff.

"Good." I sipped my tea. "Is it wrong of me that I wish someone would slip a shiv between his ribs in the shower?"

Thompson gave a surprised laugh. "Wow."

I scowled and set my chopsticks down. "I hate the guy. I'm not going to lie. He's an evil abomination. I wish he'd just disappear."

"I agree. I just don't usually say it out loud." He smirked and took a mouthful of steamed rice.

"You're a cop. You can't say that out loud. But I can."

He grunted. "Percy is probably going to end up in a psych ward."

"Well, he isn't all there."

"I keep wondering why you couldn't get a sense of guilt off of Percy for the murders? Was Pine blocking you?"

"I think so. And technically, Percy didn't kill the girls. Pine did. I mean... Percy committed the murders, but it was Pine at the helm."

"Except for Shalondra's murder. That was all Percy."

"True." I sighed. "It's confusing. I won't pretend otherwise. All I know is, I couldn't read his guilt."

"Yeah, a lot of things were confusing about this case. It didn't help any that people kept hiding shit."

"Or just accidentally leading us astray. Like when Valerie used the name 'Rusty.' I thought she meant it literally, but it was her nickname for Percy because of his red hair."

"I should have believed you from the start when you said you thought Pine was involved." He sighed. "I should always listen to your instincts."

"He was locked away. It seemed far-fetched."

He chuffed. "Far-fetched or not, from now on I'll believe your hunches."

"I still find it nuts that someone who started a suicide prevention group was involved in killing some of the members." I met his gaze. "Do you think Percy started the group with the intention of letting Pine pick them off one by one?"

"I don't. Percy started the group before he started corresponding with Pine. I think that was just Pine taking advantage. Percy started that group seeking support because of his own suicidal thoughts. Pine saw it as an opportunity to continue his twisted work."

I shivered. "I can't believe Percy thought Pine was a genius. What is wrong with that kid?"

"People are weird."

"Amen."

We ate in silence for a while, and then he finished off his beer and set the glass down with a bump. I could see tension in his jaw, and I waited for him to speak. "So have you thought about my living together suggestion?"

My stomach tightened. "You mean about who gives up their place?"

"Yes."

"I've definitely thought about it." I pressed my napkin to my lips, feeling anxious. I didn't know how to express my melancholy at the idea of giving up the house I'd shared with Will. Even though I understood how Thompson felt, it seemed wrong. But I wanted to live with Thompson, and I didn't want to do anything that ruined that.

"I've thought about it a lot too." He grimaced. "I initially really didn't want to move into your place. I'm sure you could feel that." He didn't meet my gaze. "Even though Will and I were like brothers, it felt weird and wrong for whatever reason to move into his house. But then I realized I was being selfish."

I squinted. "Really?"

"That's your home. You and Will put down roots there. You picked that house with care, and you planned on living there the rest of your days. The part I was stuck on was you planned that future with Will. Not me. I felt like if I moved in, I was almost disrespecting Will." He gave a gruff laugh.

"I don't see it that way."

He glanced up, his eyes warm with affection. "I don't either. Not anymore. I could tell the idea of leaving that house hurt you. But I was too much in my head at first. The more I thought about it, the more I knew what the right thing was. I never planned on living where I am forever. I don't care where I live, so long as you're there and I can bring Sparkles with me."

Relief rippled through me. "Well, you have to bring Sparkles." My voice wobbled as I fought to contain my emotions. "I think she might even be warming up to me. I thought she said she loved me the other day… although she might have been talking to the TV."

He smiled and reached across the table, covering my hand with his. "I can't promise that what you had with Will won't occasionally intimidate me." He sighed. "But I trust what we have together."

I scooted closer to him. "I'll always love Will. You know that. But I love you too, and I want you, Thompson. I want to be here with you. I swear."

He leaned in and kissed me softly. "Same."

We smiled at each other and then started eating again.

"I'm glad we have that settled," he said, sounding more cheerful.

I helped myself to the sushi. "When should we do this?"

"That's kind of up to you."

"Not really. It's up to us. When is your next day off?"

"Saturday."

"I'll pencil you and Sparkles in." I grinned.

"Oh, okay. I'll book a U-Haul." He grimaced. "Shit. I haven't moved in ten years. I'm out of practice."

"I can help you pack."

"Damn straight you're helping me. I'm lost." He laughed, lifting one brow. "Where do you even buy bubble wrap?"

I chuckled. "We'll figure it out."

He sighed. "Now we just have to figure out when to get you together with the rest of my clan." He bit his bottom lip as if trying not to smile.

I widened my eyes. "One thing at a time, Thompson. Come on."

His lips twitched. "I'm going to keep after you. You know that, right?"

"You're evil." My nerves rattled at the idea of meeting his whole family.

"Maybe one day... when you least expect it, you'll come back to our place and they'll all be there... waiting for you."

Shaking my head, I scowled. "You really are evil." I knew eventually I'd have to meet them, but right now I just wanted to focus on living together.

He chuckled. "I won't bring up meeting my family again until the holidays."

I breathed a sigh of relief. "Thank you."

"Hey, maybe we can invite them to our place for the Christmas?" He grinned.

"Thoommppsson." My tone held a warning.

He smirked. "Okay. Okay."

I studied him, taking in his strong yet gentle demeanor. My heart warmed at the sight of him. There was something about Thompson that soothed my soul. His energy comforted me, but also made me excited for what was to come. What I had with Thompson wasn't better or worse than what I'd had with Will. But Thompson was a part of me now. He was my world. Maybe seeing the past was my specialty, but with Thompson by my side, I wasn't afraid to leap blindly into the future.

The End

Other Books by S.C. Wynne

Hard-Ass is Here

Christmas Crush

Hard-Ass Vacation

The New Boss

Guarding My Heart

The Cowboy and the Barista

Guard My Body-Rerelease coming soon!

Damaged Heart-Rerelease coming soon!

Up in Flames

Until the Morning

The Fire Underneath

Kiss and Tell

Secrets from the Edge

Hiding Things

Home to Danger

Assassins Are People Too #1

Painful Lessons

Assassins Love People Too #2

Believing Rory

Unleashing Love

Starting New

The Cowboy and the Pencil-Pusher

Memories Follow

My Omega's Baby Book One

Rockstar Baby Book Two

Manny's Surprise Baby Book Three

Bodyguards and Babies Box Set

Mistletoe Omega

Falling Into Love #1

Shadow's Edge Book One

Buy Links for all my books are available at www.sc-wynne.com

Copyright (c) 2018 by S.C. Wynne

Shadow's Return Book Two

March 1 2018

Edited by Sandra Depukat (One Love Editing)

This is a work of fiction. Any resemblance to persons

living or dead is entirely coincidental.

Made in the USA
Las Vegas, NV
18 March 2022

45924541R10144